Cinnamon and Nutmeg

CINNAMON AND NUTMEG

by
Anne de Roo

7612
F
DER   TITLE II

THOMAS NELSON INC.
NASHVILLE / NEW YORK

No character in this story is intended to represent any actual person; all the incidents of the story are entirely fictional in nature.

Copyright © 1972, 1974 by Anne de Roo

All rights reserved under International and Pan-American Conventions. Published by Thomas Nelson Inc., Nashville, Tennessee. Manufactured in the United States of America.

First U.S. edition

Library of Congress Cataloging in Publication Data

De Roo, Anne.
  Cinnamon and Nutmeg.

  SUMMARY: A young girl growing up on an Australian farm finds two orphans in the bush, a kid and a newborn calf, and tries to take care of them secretly.
  [1. Farm life—Australia—Fiction. 2. Animals—Fiction.
3. Australia—Fiction] I. Title.
PZ7.D446Ci3   [Fic]   73–19939
ISBN 0–8407–6372–7

For John

Contents

Cinnamon and Nutmeg

ONE

The Farm-Boy Daughter

If she had not been in a bad mood already, Tessa would have waited, as she usually did, until the four Howarth children had pushed and shrieked their way out of the school bus before she left her seat. But she was too miserable to be patient. She joined in their scramble, shoving her way down the steps between Billy and Carol, until a thump on the back sent her sprawling forward to land on both knees on the road.

"You did that on purpose," she told Warren, the biggest and roughest of the Howarths.

"Who, me? I never. Musta been your fatful old dog. Your old dog full of fat."

Billy, Carol, and Charlie screamed with laughter at a joke which, not being in Tessa's class, they could not possibly understand. From inside the bus she heard Vivienne Ritchie, who was her cousin and supposedly her friend, giggle wildly, and then like a chorus the rest of the busload of children joined in. She turned her back on them and limped off toward home while Warren swung on the Howarths' gate and chanted after her, "Fatful old dog."

It was the title of a story Tessa had written that Jenny Wren—Miss Jennifer Renfrew, who taught the fifth and sixth grade at Manurima School—had read out to the whole class. Only the title. There had been a time when the whole of Tessa's stories had been read out because they were good. But that was before Miss Renfrew came to teach at Manurima School.

"Fatful"—Tessa would have been ashamed without a public reading. The story of the faithful old dog was the most important story she had ever written because it was the true story of Sport, her father's old cattle dog, who had been her friend as long as she could remember and who had died only last week. She had written it as homework and had torn three pages out of her exercise book because they were blotted with tears.

After the class had stopped laughing and settled down to work, Jenny Wren had demanded an explanation of this "wanton destruction." Pale-blue eyes in a pale face, between shoulder-length curtains of blond hair—there was a blue and white calm about Jenny Wren that reminded Tessa of pictures she had seen of ice and snow. She ruled the class with a sarcasm that left Warren Howarth and his friends unmoved but made Tessa so nervous that she tried as she had never tried before and somehow only succeeded in making mistakes as stupid as "fatful" for "faithful."

Her grazed knees began to sting and blood trickled down the inside of her socks. She reached the boundary between Mr. Howarth's land and her father's. Across the barbed-wire fence she could see a grazing herd of Jersey cows and behind them, through a gap in a row of macrocarpa trees, the cream-painted wooden bungalow that was home, where plump, reliable Mum shuffled about in the kitchen in worn slippers, bustling around to have a cup of tea ready when Tessa came home. She imagined she was a sailor on just such a rough, raw winter afternoon and that the little wooden house was her home port. It was Friday. For two days she would shelter from the storms of Jenny Wren's sarcasm, helping Dad around the farm all day, with Mum always there to provide safety and food and warmth.

"Tessa!" She had scarcely noticed her father's old Ford truck until it pulled up on the roadside opposite her and Dad's head leaned out the window. "Tessa, I'm just taking your mother . . ."

He did not need to say more. Tessa had known for days that the new baby might arrive at any time. But it was making a bad start as a member of her family to choose a time when she had such a need of her mother.

Mum smiled at her from the other side of Dad, her face as round and red and untroubled as usual. "Look after your father like a good girl, won't you. There's all the food you'll need in the refrigerator and plenty of bread and cake. You'd better call your Uncle Alec and ask him to help with the milking, in case Dad isn't back in time. Don't forget to feed the fowls. And be a good girl. Pity Ruthie isn't home."

"I can manage," said Tessa stiffly. She did not want to be reminded that she was a less useful daughter than Ruth.

Mum leaned across to pat the white knuckles of the hand that clutched the edge of the open window. "I know you can manage," she said. "Ruth would have been company for you, that's all." But Tessa knew that was not what she had been thinking.

She stood waving until the truck was lost around a bend in the road. The prospect of a baby brother or sister did not comfort her. Ruth had gone wild with joy at the news, but Tessa had never yet seen a small human being that compared in beauty or character with a baby animal. She limped toward the house.

In the big kitchen where they chiefly lived a kettle was steaming on the edge of the stove. The table was already laid for tea and covered with a cloth. Tessa lifted a corner and peeped in. There was ham and winter salad, bread,

honey, and a freshly made sponge cake. After milking she
would only have to make a pot of tea and she and her
father would sit down to a well-earned meal. They would
not talk much; they never did. It was not the amount of
talking that showed the size of their friendship.

Tessa made herself a cup of tea, took a couple of cookies
from one of the brimming cans in the pantry and sat down
to enjoy her importance as the woman of the house. Ruth
would envy her. Ruth was the domesticated one; Tessa
was the farm-boy daughter. But Ruth was away at boarding
school all term.

When she had drunk her tea she bathed her knees and
put bandages on them, telephoned Uncle Alec to ask him
to help with the milking, and changed into old jeans and
a ragged shirt and went out to get the cows. With a whole
farm in her charge she was an important person and beginning to enjoy it.

Daisy, however, was not impressed. Daisy was the most
contrary cow that Tessa had ever met. When it was not
milking time she would stand for hours with her head
over the gate, bellowing to be let through, but at milking
time she was almost always at the far end of the paddock
and determined to stay there. Sport had known all about
Daisy, and while Tessa was rounding up the meeker
cows he would ease her so gently toward the gate that
Daisy, who was not very bright, thought she was going
there by her own choice.

Now there was no Sport, and Daisy knew it. Two of the
more flighty heifers joined her in her rebellion while the
rest of the herd trailed meekly down the road toward
the cowyard. Tessa limped through the mud, first to one
corner of the paddock and then to another, after Daisy
and her two allies. They would never have dared behave
like that when Sport was alive.

At last the heifers tired of the game and Daisy, finding herself deserted, followed through the gate with a mild-eyed and reproachful glance at Tessa, as if to say that she had always intended to do just that if Tessa hadn't interfered. Like a model of good behavior she trotted down the road.

Uncle Alec and his grown-up son, Trevor, were already driving the cows into the stalls when Tessa arrived with the three stragglers.

"Been playing up?" said Trevor, grinning, as he opened the gate for them.

"They certainly have," said Tessa, returning his grin manfully, one farmer to another, although there were tears misting her eyes for Sport.

"Knows old Sport's gone." Trevor gave Daisy a slap on the rump that sent her clumping without dignity across the cowyard.

Uncle Alec was Dad's stepbrother and twenty years his senior. His back was bent with arthritis and he walked with a permanent limp. "That makes two of us," he said when he saw Tessa's limp. She was pleased at the thought of being like Uncle Alec, who of all the uncles, cousins, and second cousins who owned the small farms around Manurima, was her favorite.

"Well, Tessa," he asked much later when he and Trevor were washing the cups of the milking machine while she sloshed buckets of water over the concrete floor, "looking forward to the new baby?"

"No more washing cow stalls for you, Tessa," said Trevor. "You'll be helping bathe the baby."

"I certainly will not," said Tessa indignantly. "She'll have Mum to look after her."

"So it's going to be a girl, is it?"

Tessa nodded. She could not explain that she had made

up her mind when she first heard about the baby. When you made up your mind as firmly as that, things had to come true.

"Dad says I'm all the son he needs," she said. "He says he knows a lot of farm boys who aren't half as useful as I am."

Trevor laughed, but Uncle Alec said, "Too right, Tessa. And so I told your father when he was bragging about the son he was going to have. 'You'll be lucky to have a son that's half the farmer young Tessa is,' I told him."

Tessa liked Uncle Alec's praise but not the news that Dad was planning to have a boy.

She refused their invitation to go back with them to Uncle Alec's. Somebody had to be home to get Dad's tea. She walked to the bungalow through gathering darkness and settled down in the kitchen to wait until they could have tea together.

She tried to read but hunger and anxiety distracted her and after a while she turned to the flyleaf of her book where a girlish hand had written *Helen Duggan, her book*.

She liked thinking about Aunt Helen, who had once owned most of the books that were now her own. All Tessa's best friends, the private friends that she met in her favorite books, had once been the friends of a girl who had lived in the old house that was now Uncle Alec's. That the books had been precious to Aunt Helen was obvious from the wear of many rereadings.

But what had Helen Duggan been like? Ruth, who often on weekends visited the grown-up Aunt Helen and her daughter Jan, spoke only of their smart clothes, their lovely furniture, and the modern kitchen of their apartment. Ruth noticed things like that. And when Tessa asked Dad what his sister had really been like, he only said that she had all the brains of the family. She had left the farm to go to the university; she had crossed the world to spend most of her adult life in London. Now she lived in an apartment with a view of the sea, Ruth said, but without a green paddock in sight. It seemed a foolish choice for a woman who was supposed to be clever. Tessa could not imagine anyone wanting to live in town. Ruth did, but Ruth was silly about a lot of things.

Thinking about Aunt Helen didn't hurt. It was better than thinking about Sport or the new baby or, as the evening dragged on, about the accident that Dad might have had.

Ten struck on the front-room clock, and then, so soon after that she must have dozed off, eleven. It was past midnight when a car engine roared across the silence and then died. Footsteps came up the front path, which might be Dad's or a burglar's or a policeman's come to report an accident.

A key turned easily in the front door and strangely unsteady footsteps came down the hall. Then she heard Dad at the telephone, shouting as though he relied on his voice alone to carry his words to Uncle Alec on the next farm. "That you, Alec? Yeah, a son. Yeah, she's fine. Yeah, I been celebrating. You hear what I said? A son, Daniel, after our old man. Keep the name going, eh? Daniel Duggan's farm. The kid, what kid? Who, Tessa? She sleeps like the dead, won't wake her. Yeah, ran into the Hope boys in town, had a few drinks to celebrate. Sold me a . . . eh? Wha's that? Aw, night's young. Aw right, aw right, don't shout at a man." The receiver slammed down and he stumbled toward the kitchen.

He did not seem surprised that Tessa was not sleeping like the dead. "Hello, old son," he said thickly. He always called her "old son" because she was his farm-boy daughter. "Brought you a little present. Something to make up for Sport. Wanner see?"

"Yes, please," Tessa heard herself say through a thick fur of tiredness and bewilderment. Nothing could make up for Sport and yet it was a relief to know that in celebrating the birth of his son he had not entirely forgotten her.

She did not see him leave the room. Perhaps she had dozed off again. Then he was pushing open the door with his foot because his arms were full of black-and-white fur. He squatted down on the floor and let the fluff stretch itself out into a young cattle dog, not more than three or four months old.

Tessa flopped to the floor and held out her arms toward the pup. It whined and backed away. She crawled after it.

" 'Sname's Sam," said Dad thickly. " 'Swell bred. Hope boys sold him to me. Gran' blokes. Gran' pup." After some thought he added, "Gran' beer."

"Sam, Sam," Tessa called softly and the pup sidled up to her and sniffed at her hand. She caught him and hugged him. His whines turned to a snuffle and he began to chew her sleeve. "Oh, Dad," she said, forgetting everything except the pup, "he's the sweetest thing."

"Here, none of that sweetest thing stuff. Working dog. Gorra job to learn."

"You said he was mine."

Dad shuffled his big feet. "Manner a speaking," he muttered.

Tessa hugged the pup tightly. She had been surrounded by animals all her life, but she had never had one that was really all her own. She had loved Sport and they had worked together on the farm, but he had still been her father's dog. "I want him," she said in a voice that seemed to come from someone younger and much more spoiled than herself.

"Worra you doin' up at this hour?" her father irrelevantly replied. "Off quickly—only parent says so."

Tessa clung to Sam. "Where's he going to sleep?" she asked, and at once found her own answer. "I know, Dad, I know where there's a box and an old sweater of Mum's. I'll fix him up a bed right here in the warm kitchen and then I'll go straight to bed myself, promise."

Dad bent down and scooped up the pup. Holding it under its forelegs so that it dangled uncomfortably, he looked down at Tessa. "Kitchens!" he said. "Warm beds! Din't I tell you thissa working dog? C'mon, Sam, we'll show you how farm dogs live."

From the floor, Tessa looked up at him. He seemed immensely tall and thin, with inches of bare arm showing where his sleeves were, as usual, too short. In that, he looked like her father. But her father did not yell and slur his words; her father did not come home drunk.

Sam whined in a small voice as he was carried through the kitchen door. Then the whines turned to yelps and a chain rattled.

Tessa ran through the door that led to the sunroom where she slept. She did not want to see her father again that night.

She was too lost in her own misery to be aware for some time of the yelps and whines outside the window that rose to a crescendo of heartbroken howls. She switched on her bedhead light and listened. Her father's voice was raised in tuneless song from the other end of the house. Then it abruptly stopped. She waited but there was no further sound except the pup's steady howling.

She crept on bare feet through the outside door that was

one of the privileges of sleeping in the sunroom. Light flooded through its wide windows across the lonely little creature and the big chain that was fully stretched behind him.

She struggled frantically with the taut chain, fearing each moment that her father would be roused by the noise and come out with his strange new anger.

When at last she succeeded in releasing him, Sam bounded into the darkness. But he was instantly back again, wild with joy, to scratch at her pajama legs with muddy paws and then to run off, as if he expected her to play chasing in the dark. She was shivering and her bare feet were as numb as stones before she could get her hand through his collar and drag him into the sunroom.

She climbed into bed, switched off the light, and listened to the click of Sam's claws on the floor and the occasional bump against furniture as he blindly sniffed his way around the strange room. He began to whine again. She called to him.

With a shock like an earthquake he landed on her bed and began to lick her face.

Tessa pulled out her arms from under the weight of pup and bedclothes and dragged him down into the bed. Her father's "working cattle dog" seemed to feel that it was just the right place for him. With a final lick of her hand he stretched at full length beside her and was soon gently snoring. Tessa clung to him as, long ago and forgotten until now, she had clutched her teddy bear in times of infant misery.

TWO

A Stranger in the Bush

Mum and her baby left the hospital on Friday afternoon and at once the little farmhouse became a home again. Tessa felt it as she came in for breakfast on Saturday morning. There was frost in the air; the warmth of the kitchen after hard work outdoors set her skin tingling with a mixture of heat and cold. As she sat down at her place, where a plate of cereal was already steaming, Mum turned from the stove to smile at her. That was another kind of warmth that she had missed when she woke to a cold kitchen with Dad's breakfast to cook and a school bus to catch and Dad in a bad mood, despite his newborn son, because, however hard she tried, nothing was ever ready when he wanted it or in the right place for him. Mum always seemed to know more about what Dad needed and when he needed it than he did himself.

She hurried through her breakfast, looking forward to the moment when she could leave the kitchen in Mum's competent hands and go out to feed the calves. Usually at weekends she began feeding them before Dad, who was a slow eater, had finished his breakfast.

"And where do you think you're going?" he asked as she was pulling on her boots.

Tessa was surprised that he should ask. He must have found it a long week if he had forgotten her Saturday morning routine.

"You'll stay right here and help your mother with the dishes."

Mum gave Tessa a shy and apologetic smile across the table, but she did not argue. Tessa returned her one outdoor foot to its slipper and went to the sink, which all week had been so familiar and so hated.

She washed and dried the dishes while Mum fed Daniel. "Can I go now?" she asked hopefully when the last plate was stacked away.

Mum looked at her across the crumpled, red-faced bundle as if, Tessa thought jealously, she was surprised that the world should contain any creature but Daniel, dribbling milk from the corners of his mouth. "I wish you'd stay just a minute and make the beds and do the dusting, Tessa," she said.

When that was done, Mum wished that the kitchen floor were clean. The morning was half over before she had finished, and half a morning was a quarter of a weekend. It was almost without hope that she asked if she could take Dad's morning tea to him.

Mum smiled up from where she was cramming diapers into the washing machine. "Off you go," she said, "and tell your father you can stay if he wants you. Never mind, Tessa, Ruth will be home soon."

She said it kindly but Tessa felt like a failure.

She released Sam from his chain and together they ran across the paddocks. It was a radiant morning with the night frost gone from the air and only a light breeze to bring from the west, as subdued as a whisper, a hint under the glowing sky that winter had not quite gone.

Behind the house and the green lowland paddocks where the cows grazed, the land began to rise too steeply for dairy cows. These "back paddocks" had been cleared more than once in the hundred years since Tessa's great-grandfather bought the land, and Dad had talked often of clearing them again and running a few sheep. But he had not done so while Tessa was his "farm-boy daughter."

Tessa had more than once during the past week had a feeling of being teased, not now but during the whole six years since she first began to help on the farm. On the Monday morning after Daniel was born Dad had begun to clear the back paddocks. And he had many other plans for improving the farm. "I'm not goin' to have my son saying his old man never left him nothing but a scrubby farm and a load of debts," she had heard him tell Uncle Alec.

He was out there now, leaning on his slasher among some newly cut manuka bushes. He had visitors, Ted Howarth from the next farm and a young man Tessa had never seen before.

Tessa approached them slowly. She did not like Mr. Howarth any better than she liked his sons. He was a big, dark, sullen-looking man in jeans and boots and a checked shirt with half its buttons missing. An old felt hat, made shapeless by age and weather, was crammed on his head. She had only once seen him without his hat and that was in church for the christening of his youngest child.

The other man was much younger than Mr. Howarth and Dad. He was nearly as thin as Dad, but shorter, almost frail-looking, and Tessa thought him rather handsome. His hair was long and he had a small moustache, he seemed more like a town man than any farmer Tessa knew. There was hardly a speck of mud on his boots and his corduroy trousers and well-cut jacket looked brand new.

Sam bounded up to Dad and scraped his claws up his boots as far as he could reach. Dad ignored him and looked at Tessa. "I told you," he said, "he's a working dog, not a kid's pet."

The young man bent down and patted Sam. "Nice pup," he said, looking at Tessa. "What do you call him?"

The anger left Dad's face. He was still proud of the pup he had bought. "Bought him from the Hope boys," he said. "Good lads, those, and keep good stock. Matter of fact, they've got a nice young bull I've got my eye on too. Sired by your boss's bull and you can't do better than that."

There was only one bull in the district that he would speak of with such respect, the one from the famous Riverlea herd. In that case, thought Tessa, who as farm boy knew all the farmers' gossip, the young man must be the new farm manager of Riverlea, her cousin Pat Duggan, known as Young Pat because his father, Dad's step-brother, who had left the district before she was born, was also called Pat.

"Aw, I dunno," mumbled Mr. Howarth. "Pedigree stock, prizes at all the shows. Don't count for much if you ask me. I reckon the Riverlea herd's just a rich man's toy."

"You come and take a look at our butterfat figures, Ted," said Young Pat amiably. "See how they compare with the yield from those walking scarecrows of yours."

Mr. Howarth flushed. He had no reason to be proud of his patchwork herd of Jerseys and Jersey-crosses or the neglected land that inadequately fed them.

"Your new boss keeping the cows then?" Dad asked Young Pat.

"If he knows he's got 'em. I tell you, Joe, that joker doesn't know as much about farming as this girl of yours. Beats me why he gave up his lawyer's job and came out here."

"He was a good man, Graham Sanderson," said Dad. That was the Mr. Sanderson who had owned the big

Riverlea sheep farm that was the richest farm in the district and who, more as a hobby than anything else, had bred pedigree Jersey cows. A few months ago he had died and the land had been inherited by his younger brother, Mr. Dennis Sanderson. Tessa had not met the younger Mr. Sanderson but she had heard the farmers talk of him. Some thought him a good joke, while others, her father among them, were angry that a man who had not been on a farm since boyhood should own the best land and the finest stock in the district.

"If you're looking for Riverlea blood, Joe," said Young Pat, "we've got a nice young bull for sale."

"No holding him back since he's got a son," said Mr. Howarth with an unpleasant laugh. "He'll be wanting to buy Riverlea Princess next." Princess stood out among the Riverlea cows as they stood above the other cows of the district.

Tessa listened eagerly to their conversation. She pictured the sleek daughters of the Riverlea bull and then herself, leading a heifer around the show ring as she had seen Mr. Graham Sanderson lead his cows, its neck swathed in prize ribbons. And as a practical farmer she saw the yellow, butter-rich milk flowing into the milking bucket. "Please, Dad, do buy a Riverlea bull," she said, her hazel eyes round with the glory of their future.

The two men laughed, but Dad did not laugh with them. His eye had again caught the delinquent pup, lying across Tessa's foot and chewing a stick. "All I want from you, missy, is a bit of obedience. Have your cup of tea and then take that dog of mine straight back to his kennel."

"I don't want any tea. Give it to your friends." Tessa was angry at being treated like a child in front of the other farmers.

As she turned away she heard Young Pat say, "There's

the Duggan temper, eh, Joe?" But she didn't care about the Duggan temper or the bad manners that were all her own. Dad was unfair both to herself and Sam and she was not going to work on his farm.

She was not going to be involved in any more housework either. She ran home, crept into her sunroom by its private door, took a book from the bookcase and, with Sam still beside her, strolled back across the paddocks to Grandpa Pat's house.

The crumbling wooden house stood in a steep and scrubby paddock toward the back of the farm. Except for the homestead at Riverlea it was the only house in the district that had two stories. The two houses had, in fact, been built at the same time, but, whereas Riverlea was still inhabited, Grandpa Pat's house had never been finished and had never been lived in.

There had once been two young men who came to the uninhabited forest that was Manurima. One was Tessa's great-great-grandfather, still known to his descendants as Grandpa Pat, the other Jeremiah Sanderson, the great-grandfather of the present owner of Riverlea. Between them they bought, at a ridiculously low price even in those days, the whole of what was then called the Manurima Block. It was rugged land, not to be compared with the newly settled lands of the Taranaki plain which it bordered. It was deep in mile upon mile of uncleared bush, and neither man had any farming experience whatever, either in the old country or the new.

They intended to grow rich from the sale of wool, as others were beginning to do in the dry hill country of the south. But the warm wet hills of Taranaki were death to their long-wooled merino flocks. Both men were poor, but Grandpa Pat on the lower and damper land was the poorer of the two.

With the first refrigerated ships in the 1880's they saw

new opportunities. Mr. Sanderson began to run shorter-wooled, sturdier sheep which could now be shipped to England as frozen lamb, while Grandpa Pat, who had long since lost all faith in sheep, increased his herd of dairy cows, for butter could also be sent overseas on the new ships.

Jeremiah Sanderson began to build a fine homestead at Riverlea; Grandpa Pat began to build a house that must be as fine as his neighbor's. Each year Mr. Sanderson grew richer and employed more men to work for him and did less work himself, while Grandpa Pat worked early and late, hand-milking his herd of cows, driving his horse and cart down mud tracks to deliver the cream to the dairy factory with only his own large family to help him.

Riverlea homestead was completed and lived in for many years before Grandpa admitted defeat. Work on his house was stopped and started again many times before at last it stopped forever. All over Grandpa Pat's great holding, on farms just big enough to support one man and his family, his descendants lived in unimpressive wood or brick bungalows, and still Grandpa Pat's house stood, half built and crumbling, in its overgrown paddock.

Tessa and Ruth were forbidden to enter the house because of the danger of falling timber, but the wide veranda that had stood firm against eighty years of wind and rain was their private retreat. They had two armchairs there, with broken springs and horsehair and webbing dangling from them. Ruth's even had a charred cushion that she had rescued one day after Mum had thrown it on a bonfire.

Tessa sat down on her lumpy chair while Sam climbed onto Ruth's and began to fight a battle with the cushion. She opened the book that she had snatched at random from the bookcase.

By good luck she had picked up *Huckleberry Finn,* which

she had not read for six months and which seemed just the right book for her mood. It would serve Dad right if she did sail away on a raft like Huck and Jim or, since the only river available, the little Waipuke which flowed out of the bush and across Riverlea, was not at all like the Mississippi as she imagined it, it would serve him right if she just walked away on her own two feet. But since such real adventures could only be a dream, she settled down to live adventurously on the distant Mississippi.

She had meant to be home in time to help with lunch. She had meant to keep an eye on Sam and the cushion, too. But when she looked up from her book the cushion was in shreds, and when she reached home Mum and Dad were already sitting eating at the kitchen table. Neither of them made any comment, even when Sam bounded with muddy paws across the clean kitchen floor.

After lunch Dad said, "Tessa, if you can't be home when you're wanted, at least you can stay and do the dishes while your mother has a rest."

Afternoon rests had been an unwilling part of Mum's routine in the few months before Daniel was born, but Tessa had supposed that life would return to normal now, in that respect at least. Daniel seemed to have changed nothing, except for the worse.

And then, perhaps because she was thinking more of her own troubles than of what she was doing, Mum's best vegetable dish, the last of the set that Grandma and Grandpa Ritchie had given her as a wedding present, slipped through her fingers and smashed into a dozen pieces on the floor.

Tessa gathered up the pieces and took them out to the garbage can. The confession to come weighed heavily as she tramped back to Grandpa Pat's house with her work-basket in her hand. Mum was usually fair about an honest accident honestly reported, but she had loved that vegetable dish. Ruth's cushion and Mum's vegetable dish— why, Tessa wondered, pitying herself more than the people who had lost them, did it have to be people's most precious possessions that she destroyed?

Five minutes' work with needle and thread showed her that the cushion was beyond her aid. It was probably beyond the skill even of Ruth's fingers. *Huckleberry Finn* still lay on the veranda, but she no longer felt like reading. She called Sam and, keeping well clear of the paddock where Dad was working, headed toward the back of the farm.

The little farm was tucked, cozily, Tessa always thought, under the shelter of a long range of hills. There were no boundary fences, just bush that nobody had cleared. Tessa did not know if anybody owned the hills. She doubted it. They had the look of hills that belonged only to themselves and whichever Maori gods still lurked among them.

At a deep pool among the trees, where she and Ruth went swimming in summer, she stood a long time, gazing at the still water. The thick roof of the rain forest was divided by the river, and a band of sunlight broke through to point its depths with amber and green. The water stirred only when an occasional dead leaf or twig dropped from an overhanging tree. Between the bustle of white rapids above and below, the pool lay like a mirror in which was reflected not her own face but shining green and brown rocks with a drift of waterweed trailing in an invisible current.

At last she called to Sam and set off along the riverbank. There was no track beyond the pool, and to wander into the bush was forbidden. Nor would Tessa at any

other time have been so foolish as to try. The trees grew
thickly and the little space between them was a tangle
of saplings, ferns, and creepers, littered with rotting tree
trunks.

At first Tessa tried to follow the river, but she soon
found it easier to take such paths through the undergrowth as briefly opened up. Only the calls of the bush
birds and Sam's whines as he pushed through the undergrowth kept her company. Beyond was the great presence of the bush itself, windless and richly smelling of
decay, stretching ahead of her whichever way she turned
and, above her head, securely roofed by the intertwining
branches of tall trees. It was a place where one might easily
get lost. And to get lost was just what Tessa intended.

She had thought it over as she stood beside the pool.
No one was going to pay attention to her as long as she
did right. And if she did wrong they would only get
angry. But if they lost her, even if it was through her own
disobedience, then they'd care. Parents always did in
books.

She would not, of course, get too lost, not so completely
that search parties would have to be sent into the bush,
not so completely that she and Sam would die of starva-
tion. Already she could see the joy on Dad's face when
she was found. She could not believe that he had stopped
loving her completely because of Daniel.

It was all very clear to Tessa as she pushed through the
trees. And yet it was more like reading a book about
Tessa Duggan than living her life. In the story she had
told herself there was no dark or cold or hunger to be
lived through, only a happy ending.

Reality came with a big crash and a breaking of
branches that came straight toward her out of the silent
trees. Some sort of large animal was pushing through the

undergrowth. Not a wild goat—goats were small and dainty. A wild pig then? A savage boar with long tusks, like the one Dad had shot when he went pig hunting as a young man, which before it was killed, had slashed a pig dog in a way that always made Tessa cover her ears when Dad came to that part of the story.

As the animal blundered toward them Sam ran yapping forward. He was too small and nimble to be caught, too excited to remember his few lessons in obedience. Tessa in a panic gave up her pursuit and swung herself into the lowest fork of a tree. As she began to climb she heard below, as if in a dream, the safe, familiar moo of a cow.

The creature pushed through the last thicket and stood directly under Tessa's tree, tossing her head in a manner more bewildered than ferocious. A little Jersey cow. She stayed long enough for Tessa's farm-boy eyes to take in the beauty of her, the long sloping body, slender legs, and glossy coat the color of bush honey. And that she was in calf. For a moment she looked up at the girl in the tree as if at another part of an adventure to be endured with only a timid question, just a mild glance that seemed to ask, "Why should this happen to me?" Then she meekly trotted forward, driven by an ecstatic Sam, as if that too must be accepted, but with dignity, like a queen, Tessa thought—lost in the wilderness and harassed by a mischievous urchin, but with all her royal dignity still.

By the time she had climbed down from the tree the cow's progress could be heard only as a distant crackling of branches. Sam, wagging not only his tail but his whole body with delight and the expectation of praise, greeted her. She dared not follow the cow farther into the bush. She might get lost.

That anybody should go out into the bush on purpose

to get lost was unbelievable. She had looked into the eyes of an animal that was truly lost. All that was sensible in Tessa, which was most of her, looked back in amazement at the girl who had set out to punish her parents by getting lost in the bush. That was not the Tessa Duggan she knew and she was frightened, as if she had found a stranger lurking in her own personality, frightened of the results that still might come from that other Tessa's reign. For although she had not gone far into the bush, all directions looked and sounded alike.

It was strange, when from out on the open farm the bush-covered hills could be seen to rise steeply, how little evidence of rising ground the bush itself offered. The river could give the only possible clue to direction, but it was not easy to reach the river even when at last she heard the sound of its rapids. Several times she lost it again, drew close and was forced away by crowding undergrowth. And then, suddenly, when she thought she had lost it forever, she was standing on its bank, not in a place she knew, perhaps far yet from the familiar swimming hole, but at least with some guide, something distinct from the changeless pattern of trees.

THREE

The Orphans

Tessa sat down on a claybank and rested her feet on a boulder to keep them from the thick black mud that formed an evil-smelling beach at the river's edge. She had the river to follow home, but she still trembled with panic and tiredness.

On the other side of the river a hill rose steeply with bulges of gray rock face breaking through the green of the bush. Tall rocks stood at the river's edge and behind them Tessa could just make out a black curve which appeared to be the roof of a cavern. It might be no more than a small hollow under the hill or it might be the entrance to some grand and gloomy underground chamber. It might be a Maori burial cave, full of painted bones and protected by a taboo to bring sickness or death to anyone who entered. She had heard of such caves in these hills, and rising so black against the amber river, it looked like a place of death.

Something small and dark moved among the rocks. Tessa leaped to her feet and landed half up her boots in mud. She looked down at them and when a moment later she looked again at the opposite bank, the thing had vanished. But Sam had seen it too. He looked across the river and whined and the hair on his back rose stiffly.

Tessa, with fingers of fear drumming icily against her spine, waded step by step through the mud. Under the shallow river lay a firm bed of stones. As she paused there to watch gray clouds of mud from her boots drift away like dawn mist, Sam crossed the river in a frantic dog paddle and disappeared among the rocks from where, a moment later, his voice was raised in excited, staccato yaps. Whatever it was had been small and spindly. It had not looked dangerous, but still, as Tessa crossed the river, her skin bristled with fear as if it did not agree with the decision of her mind.

From the top of the rocks she found herself looking down into a fertile trough where young plants fought for space in a tangle of bright green. Above them the cavern mouth rose high. It was scarcely a cave at all; she could see right through to the back, across heaps of boulders, scattered by a long-past rockfall and now mossy with ferns growing up in the cracks.

Among the rocks Sam, sleek as a seal with river water, was alternately barking and whining at a spindly-legged, wobbly kid.

It could not have been more than a week old, as young as Daniel, who lay wrapped in his bedclothes and never exerted himself except to wail for his mother when he was hungry or uncomfortable. Daniel, faced with the noisy monster that Sam must appear to the kid, would not even have realized the danger, for he knew only sleep and milk and the noise that demanded his mother's attention. The kid, however, recognized danger and, to the limits of its weakness, faced it. It lowered its tiny hornless head and advanced unsteadily toward the pup. Sam, himself young and inexperienced, was impressed; his bark grew louder but there was a note of hysteria to it.

As Tessa scrambled across the rocks the kid looked up. The size of the new intruder and the rattle of falling stones were too much for its precocious courage. With a small bleat of terror it turned and vanished into the undergrowth. Tessa just succeeded in catching Sam's collar as he set off in pursuit, his fear lost in the delight of a moving quarry.

He jumped and choked against her grip as Tessa followed as quietly as she could into the tangle of young growth. She went forward reluctantly. She did not want to see the sight she guessed at, but her farm training had instilled in her the belief that a young animal must be saved, whatever the cost.

In the cave mouth, where young trees had hidden it when she looked down from above, lay a goat, its hair the same dark brown as the kid's. The kid itself was huddled against its side, trembling, waiting for the protection that all young things have a right to expect. But there was no more protection. The filmed eyes looked straight at Tessa but they did not see her. Above them the dark hair was matted and Tessa could see the small hole where the bullet had entered.

She squatted down as close as she dared with her hand held out and her voice speaking random, gentle words. She longed to snatch the kid up in her arms and force comfort upon it, but she knew she must wait. Trust must be learned, not taken by force.

She waited motionless, until her legs were aching under her, and at last the kid, finding its mother deaf to all its cries and accustomed to the still figure in the cave mouth, stepped forward and sniffed at her hand. It had to learn about the world on its own now and did not realize that Tessa belonged to the species of animal that had killed its mother, not for food or clothing but for the fun of killing. It crept closer, its little brown nose like wrinkled leather, sniffing at the human smell. The smell was strange but not frightening.

Its long neck stretched out. "Suck," its instinct told it, urgently, for its mother had been dead many hours, and the small lips found the one thing they could grasp that was warm and soft, Tessa's finger.

She let it suck while her free hand stroked its neck. "Nutmeg," she said softly and smiled to herself that after a week as housewife she should see colors in terms of the kitchen cupboard even when surrounded by large matters of life and death that were far removed from the busy, practical routine of the kitchen. But the kid was the color of nutmeg, and it is always easier to make friends with somebody who has a name. "Nutmeg, little Nutmeg, what are we going to do with you, little one?"

The kid leaned against her. She could feel its thin sides moving like bellows. Nutmeg would join her mother in only a few hours unless somebody helped her. And in all the wide bush there was only Tessa who could help.

There had never been a problem in her life before that she could not take to Dad. But Dad would ask, "What were you doing in the bush?" To have been there at all was disobedience, to give the real reason was impossible. Mum would only say, "Tessa, you really shouldn't," from the surface of a mind preoccupied with Daniel, and although she might not be interested enough to be angry, she would not be any help either.

She must face up to Dad, Tessa told herself, but not yet. Both Nutmeg's life and her own reputation would be safer if Nutmeg could be found beside the swimming hole. She took a few steps forward. Nutmeg bleated at the loss, then slowly followed. Tessa was accepted as a mother goat.

Over the rocks and across the river: it was not an easy journey for a young and starving animal, mountain goat though she was. She seemed unsurprised when her new mother stretched out human hands to steady her. Sam startled her at first. But Sam was growing up as a farm dog. Once he had learned that he was not required to drive this new and strange piece of livestock, he was content to follow along quietly, ears pricked for any new command.

Nutmeg's thin sides were heaving desperately when they reached the swimming hole. She was too exhausted to bleat, but as Tessa with young branches and fern fronds made a bed for her, the soft eyes looked continually into her face as if to ask without blame the meaning of the strange and painful world into which she had been born.

"I'm not going to tell Dad," Tessa suddenly said aloud to her two companions. Sam looked up at her with his head on one side, as if trying to catch some of the few words of human speech that he recognized.

It was as if Tessa could see herself growing. One moment there was a girl who always depended on her father, the next a person with a life of her own, grown up and independent enough to cope with a secret and by her own efforts to save a young animal's life.

She hurried home. The kitchen was empty and she could hear the cows in the cowyard. A stab of guilt acknowledged that she was late for milking and that Mum would be interrupting her busy life to help with the work that was really Tessa's. There would be trouble later, but they would understand when at last she was ready to show them the healthy animal she had rescued alone.

There was a good supply of milk in the kitchen. She heated as much as her mother's largest saucepan would hold and poured it into a bucket. How much milk did a young kid need? Would cow's milk be acceptable? It was with such nervous questions that she was occupied as she plodded once more the full length of the farm.

She had boiled the milk and it was still warm when she reached the swimming hole. She gave Nutmeg two fingers

dipped in milk to suck as she had seen Dad do when he
started new calves on bucket feeding. Nutmeg sucked
greedily. Then gently Tessa pushed the small head into
the bucket. Nutmeg lapped steadily until the last drop
was gone. It was as easy as that.

Tessa sat down on a fallen tree trunk to watch in contentment as Nutmeg slept in her bed and Sam lay with
his head on Tessa's foot. While the sunlight shot the green
leaves overhead with threads of gold, she was content to
sit beside the river with the two young animals. But when
the leaves were suddenly blackened by nightfall and the
river was gray and ghostly, the trees creaked with strange
noises that she had not heard by day. Birds broke off their
song, cooed and fluttered in the trees and then were still.
Tessa tucked Nutmeg's bed around her as warmly as she
could and went home, a grubby girl who had been where
she should not have been at a time when she should not
have been out at all.

Mum had found the pieces of her vegetable dish hidden
with evident dishonesty in the garbage can. It was not a
pleasant evening. But most of the anger missed its mark,
for Tessa was still thinking of her pretty little dark brown
Nutmeg curled in her branch-and-fern nest.

Jenny Wren was not pleased with the yawning, half-
asleep state in which Tessa arrived at school each morning for the next fortnight. But her sarcasm left Tessa
unmoved. She was happy. Each morning at sunrise she was
up and out into the bush with Sam beside her. And there
would be Nutmeg, sometimes waiting impatiently beside
the river, at others just rising from her fern bed. Each
afternoon Tessa would toss her schoolbag into the sunroom and throw off her school clothes and then, in old
working clothes, hurry out to the bush for a precious half

hour with Nutmeg before it was time to bring the cows in. Often the half hour stretched itself out well into milking time, but Tessa scarcely noticed and Dad made no complaint.

It was a hard life, but she was content with its rewards as she watched the kid grow almost before her eyes from a helpless orphan to an alert and gay young animal who loved nothing better than to tease clumsy, good-natured Sam with her mock attacks. Nutmeg was gay, she was self-sufficient, and yet she was so very young. Tessa returned home to look with scorn at the helpless Daniel.

On the last Wednesday before the August holidays she took Nutmeg's afternoon feed out to the swimming hole as usual, and as usual Nutmeg was waiting on the river bank, bleating impatiently. She was doing so well that Tessa hoped to wean her soon and take from her conscience the daily burden of stolen milk. And then? she wondered as she squatted beside the kid, watching her lap up the milk. Would Nutmeg, independent, return to the bush and the free life of a wild goat? Tessa thought she had no right to stop her if that was the life she chose.

Sam snuffled around the clearing, seeking the smell of adventure. And then he found something. His whines and yaps told Tessa that the something was alive and possibly dangerous to pups and that it was hidden in a tight clump of saplings. She knew Sam too well to be alarmed by the note of fear in his voice. Anything that was new to Sam he suspected of danger, and there were still many harmless things that were new to Sam. Only the day before a very small hedgehog had produced the same mixture of alarm and curiosity.

She left Nutmeg to finish her meal alone and went

over to Sam. His tail thumped slowly with a welcome and a
question as he pressed close beside her, letting her face the
danger and yet at the same time eager to claim his own
discovery if it proved harmless and fit to chase. Tessa
knelt down and peered into the leafy growth, then carefully lifted a branch to reveal a little cave formed within
the ring of saplings.

There, curled among the leaves, was a calf, a thin,
shivering little creature that watched the girl and the
pup with big brown eyes that were dull with fear. Tessa
stretched out her hand. The calf cringed away as if the
hand were a threat. Tessa gently stroked with one hand
its dry nose while with the other she explored the protruding ribs and backbone. The calf was like a skeleton
wrapped in a fragment of reddish-brown cowhide. It
stretched out its neck and made a low, unhappy sound
that was more a groan than a moo.

Tessa left it unwillingly and searched about, urging
Sam to behave like a cattle dog and find the cow. He did
seem to try. They hunted through the clearing and along
the riverbank and through the bush as far as Tessa dared
go. She was sure she knew the cow she was seeking, the
beautiful honey-gold creature to which, absorbed in Nutmeg, she had scarcely given a thought in the last two
weeks.

From time to time Sam returned to whine beside the
thicket where the calf lay. He was right. The calf needed
their help. No living mother would leave it lying there, no
living mother would have left it so skeleton thin.

Tessa went back to the calf and tried to raise it to its
feet but it was either too weak or too frightened to stand.
She tried to drag it out of the undergrowth but could see
that she was only frightening it.

She must tell Dad. It would mean telling him every-thing, about the lost cow, about Nutmeg, and about the milk she had been stealing for more than two weeks. He would be furious, but with the patience she had seen him give many an ailing calf, a patience that was never seen in him at other times, he would save the little animal.

"Come on, Sam, run for your life!" They tore across the farm, crashing through the scrub of the top paddocks. A red-and-gold sunset was gloriously setting the hills on fire but Tessa scarcely noticed it. "Cinnamon," she panted to Sam. "Nutmeg and now Cinnamon." Dad would save the calf and, because she had found it, it would be her very own. It would grow up as beautiful as the honey-gold cow which must now be lying, like Nutmeg's mother, no longer beautiful, somewhere in the bush. Tessa looked back at the darkening trees. Something out of the bush stalked her imagination and she shivered—death and the threat of death.

Tessa climbed the cowyard fence. The cows were all out in the yard and the whine of the separator came from the little room off the cowstalls. Tessa and Sam ran to the door.

"Dad!" she called above the noise of the separator.

He turned to her a face that was angry and grew angrier as he saw them both.

"Dad," panted Tessa, "in the bush—"

"The bush? I'll give you the bush, my girl. Now, listen, Tessa, this has gone far enough. I've put up with lateness, I've put up with you dragging that dog of mine off without as much as by your leave, I've put up with you moping around the place as if you're half asleep, but I will not have you strolling in here when all the work's been done, calmly talking about the bush. Do you think your mother and I have nothing better to do than drop everything and do your work as well as our own because you're mooning about in the bush with my dog?"

"But, Dad—"

"Don't you but Dad me, my girl. I've had enough of your behavior, and if it hadn't been for your mother I'd have said all this a week ago. What's happened to you, Tessa? You used to be a pleasure to have about the place."

"Why won't you listen?"

"You'll do the listening, my girl, instead of being fresh."

"I'm not being fresh."

"I'll say what's fresh and what isn't."

He was shouting now and Tessa shouted back, but not about the urgent needs of a small Jersey calf. "You're just a slave driver! I'm always working for you, getting the cows in, working the separator, cleaning out, feeding the calves. I never have time to play like other girls do. I wish I had a father who cared. I wish you weren't my father!"

Dad slammed a bucket of skim milk on the floor, slopping it over the concrete to the delight of the lean cats that always haunted the cowstalls at milking time. "Go and help your mother get the tea. Go on. I can finish up here now I've done most of the work myself."

Tessa just stood there. She had been late for milking, she had been sleepy, but Dad had said nothing. And she had been grateful for the friendship that had kept him silent when all the time he had just been obeying Mum. She was too hurt and too angry to be sorry yet for the things she had said, but she knew that bad temper was not a luxury she could afford. She needed his friendship now more than she had ever needed it because of Cinnamon. "I'll drive the cows back," she said in little more than a whisper.

"You'll do as you're told." Dad picked up a long stick

that leaned against the barn wall and looked so tall and angry that she thought for a moment he was going to strike her. Then he turned and flicked the nearest cow sharply across the rump.

Tessa watched him drive the cows through the gate and out on the black road. She took a step to follow him but dared not. After the things that she had said and he had said, she could not confess to the unreported stray cow, the stolen milk, the secret journeys to the bush. She could not confide in him as if he were the father she had worked beside all these years. She was nothing to him now; it was all Daniel.

The farm already supported one orphan, a day-old calf whose mother had died in giving it birth. Tessa found the milk that her father had put aside for its evening feed. In its first three days a calf needed the special milk of a cow that had newly calved. She looked apologetically at the farm cats. If Dad noticed the change in the level of the feeding bucket it was they who would get the blame.

It was black night as she trudged back toward the bush. Her father's big flashlight, which she had taken from its ledge in the separator room, swung down tunnels of blackness, outlining with a ripple of gold the fronds of ferns and the young leaves of saplings. A bird cried out in its sleep and from somewhere in the depths of the bush a morepork hooted a ghostly answer.

The calf still lay curled in her little green cave. Tessa knelt down to feed her with confidence in the technique that had succeeded so well with Nutmeg. She held out her milky fingers. Cinnamon sniffed them and then turned away. She tried again and again until at last, as if bored by her insistence, the calf gave a little uninterested nibble. When she took her hand away there was no milk left. But there was no chance of getting Cinnamon to drink out of the bucket when she still lay curled inside the thicket. Tessa dipped her fingers again and again into the milk and each time the calf sucked. Again and again, until her fingers ached. When at last Cinnamon's head was firmly turned from her, she could see where the level of milk had gone down, but so very little.

There was nothing to do but give up and go home. Tessa reached into the thicket and piled up dead leaves and fern fronds as a nest for the calf, who now lay with closed eyes, her heaving sides the only indication of life. At the other nest, where Nutmeg was already sleeping, Tessa stooped and rubbed her head against the coarse goat hair. She felt grateful to Nutmeg for being there as proof that she could save a young animal without Dad's help.

When she reached home Mum and Dad had finished tea and her own was waiting in the oven. Neither of them spoke while she ate it, although she could see the anger shadowing Dad's face like thunderclouds building up. When she had washed her few dishes Mum said, without looking up from her knitting, "Bedtime, Tessa."

If there had been only Mum, Tessa would have argued that she had homework to do, but, although Dad seemed absorbed in his newspaper, she knew that any sign of argument would turn those thunderclouds into a storm of anger. She feared his anger, but even more she feared that he might ask where she had been and demand an answer. She was not going to tell, not even for Cinnamon's sake.

FOUR

Tessa Misses the School Bus

The sky was just lightening the next morning when Tessa reached the bush. The trees were an orchestra of birdsong such as she had never heard until the last two weeks, although she could not tell from their brief daytime calls which birds were singing.

At the edge of the clearing by the swimming hole she stopped with a cry that was as joyful and involuntary as any bird's, for there beside the river, on legs as wobbly as a newborn calf's, stood Cinnamon. Nutmeg, no bigger, but with a solid, elder-sister look in her steadier gait, stood nose to nose with her, sniffing at the strange animal.

At Tessa's cry Nutmeg bounded forward, bleating for milk. Tessa set down the bucket and saw the little brown nose eagerly buried in it and the tufted rudder of a tail wagging with delight before she moved on to Cinnamon and the more difficult task.

She squatted down beside the calf, dipped her fingers in the bucket and held them out. Very slowly Cinnamon walked forward, took the fingers, sucked them dry and retreated. She was frightened, but she was starving. Again she sucked and backed away, but the third time she remained beside Tessa and allowed her head to be pushed very gently into the bucket until her muzzle touched the milk. It emerged again fluffy and white and a wide pink tongue came out to give an exploratory lick. There was a measured quart in the bucket. When at last Cinnamon turned away, more than half was gone. It was little enough when the youngest calves on the farm drank six pints a day, but it was a beginning.

Tessa let Nutmeg, her own bucket licked clean, finish Cinnamon's milk. Her long tongue rolled around the edge of the empty bucket, she pushed it over and seemed to be trying to get into it, there was nothing wrong with her appetite. When there was no possibility of getting another drop she kicked up her heels so high that she seemed about to turn a somersault, then charged at Sam with lowered head so suddenly that in his surprise he did turn head over heels. He looked up at Tessa with a little questioning squeak as if to ask whether the other animal really was playing a game. Tessa did not doubt it. Joy and mischief were in every line of Nutmeg's angular body.

Above their heads the notes of the bush birds intertwined to weave a canopy of praise to the sun that was slowly threading light between the trees. The river purred on with the song it had sung all night, a song that had threatened from darkness but now had the sound of glory. Shafts of sunlight touched the white ripples on a bank of stones in midstream. It was dawn.

Nutmeg paused in her game to mouth a strip of grass that grew beside the river. As she raised her head Tessa saw a long blade hang like whiskers on each side of her mouth and then disappear. Nutmeg would soon be independent.

She led Cinnamon to a couch of moss and dead leaves, where the weak early sunlight gave a first promise of warmth. Nutmeg strutted over to investigate the newcomer, then rushed off after Sam. They would be friends in time, Tessa decided—they would all four of them be friends.

She ran all the way home for the joy of the fresh morning air. Her feet were light, her long hair flew in the wind, and she laughed aloud at Sam's looks of laughter. The day was beautiful, the day had just begun.

The familiar kitchen was transformed by her early morning adventure. Its warmth touched softly on her cold cheeks, the smell of bacon and eggs was a banquet in itself to an appetite that had flourished on morning air and exercise since before six o'clock. Tessa looked with radiant eyes at her mother, who stood at the sink washing dishes. Joy was bursting her and she could no longer keep her secret. Good-natured, smiling Mum would surely understand when both their lives were centered on caring for babies. "Mum," she began eagerly, "Mum, I—"

Mum turned from the sink to look at her. There was no smile on her face, nor was there good nature in her voice as she said, "Tessa, just look at the state you're in. Where have you been? No, you can tell me tonight," as Tessa was about to begin a more subdued account of her adventure. "Girl alive, do you realize what time it is? Wake up, Tessa."

Tessa woke up enough to look at the clock on the mantelpiece above the stove. Ten past eight. She could not possibly have been more than two hours in the bush. It had been no time at all, it had been forever, but it had not been two hours.

"Tes-SA!"

Tessa jumped.

"Tessa, go and change this minute or you'll miss the school bus."

Tessa looked again at the clock on the mantelpiece. Twelve minutes past eight. At twenty past eight the school bus stopped at the corner for Tessa and the Howarth children.

She ran to the sunroom and like a whirlwind changed

shirt and jeans for respectable schoolday blouse and
skirt. Clean white socks drove her into a fever of impa-
tience as they stuck to her hot feet. She pulled a large hole
in the leg of one but had no time to search for another
pair.

As she ran through the kitchen, scooping up a schoolbag
with one hand and her lunch with the other, her mother
said, "Tessa, your hair." Her hair felt like a bird's nest,
but there was no time for that. She almost fell against
her mother as she aimed a good-bye kiss toward her face
and rushed through the house, slamming doors as she
went. "Tes-SA!" Her mother's despairing cry just reached
her before the front door slammed.

The joy of the morning still lightened her feet as she
ran down the road, her lunch clutched in one hand, her
schoolbag trailing from the other. In the paddock beside
the house the cows grazed peacefully; the electric fence
that kept them to one end of the paddock tocked steadily
as she passed. The long, empty remainder of the paddock,
then the first of Mr. Howarth's, a bony, nondescript heifer
mooing at her over the gate, and she came around a bend
in the road to the corner where the school bus stopped.

She was just in time to see the back of the bus slide
around the corner, so close that she could recognize the
face pressed against the back window as Warren Howarth's. She waved and shouted, but if Warren saw her he
did not tell the driver.

Tessa continued to run. She was around the corner and
the bus was out of sight before she realized how useless it
was. Either she must go home and put Dad into a bad
mood by asking him to interrupt his work, get out the
truck and drive her to school, or she must walk four miles
and put Jenny Wren into a bad mood by arriving very late

indeed. Of the two she thought she preferred the anger of Jenny Wren.

She took a sandwich from her lunch box to eat on the way, pushed the box into her schoolbag, and hitched it on her shoulder. In there was untouched homework. Jenny Wren would be annoyed. While she ate her sandwich Tessa managed to feel that she was nobly suffering for her young charges in the bush. But when the sandwich was gone she was as hungry as ever and dared not take another for fear of lunchtime hunger. The bush, the birds' chorus, the young animals were as remote as something she had read long ago in a book. A four-mile walk, an angry teacher, hunger now and her lunch already one sandwich short—those were reality. Her mood swooped from joy to black misery. She could have sat down by the roadside and wept.

But, because she was Tessa Duggan and had courage, she plodded on, though so wrapped up in her own misery that the driver of the blue station wagon had to call out twice and hoot his horn before she became aware that he had pulled up beside her. "Want a lift?" she heard him call.

She wanted a lift very badly indeed but she knew better than to accept one from a strange man. And she was sure that she had never seen the driver or the station wagon before.

"You'd be one of Joe Duggan's girls," he said, half questioning, half informing her of her own identity.

Tessa hesitated only a moment longer. If the man knew her he could not be a real stranger. She hurried around to the door he had opened for her and climbed in.

"Walking to school?" he asked as the station wagon moved off.

Tessa shyly nodded.

"It's a long haul. I know. I never walked it myself but I once rode beside someone who did—your aunt it would be, of course." His voice went back into itself as adults' voices do when they remember something that happened a long time ago. "We used to ride to school, Joe your father, that is—your Aunt Peggy, your Aunt Helen, and me."

"You're Mr. Sanderson!" Tessa interrupted.

The new owner of Riverlea, the employer of her handsome cousin Young Pat, was a short, dark man, broadly built and growing rather stout about the waist, as middle-aged men do whose work involves a lot of sitting down. His eyes were small and sharp, with a fan of wrinkles at each side that gave them a kindly look. The wrinkles deepened as he said, "I am so sorry. I forgot that because I know everybody in the district, everybody doesn't know me. Now, let's start at the beginning again and get ourselves introduced. I'm Dennis Sanderson. And you, which are you, Tessa or Ruth?"

Tessa did not like the suggestion that she might be Ruth. But Mr. Sanderson had left Manurima so long before either of them was born that he could hardly be blamed for his ignorance. She informed him who she was with a touch of pride that made his eyes laugh more than ever. "Do tell me about Aunt Helen walking to school," she said. She liked to hear about the girl who had once owned her favorite books.

Mr. Sanderson looked hard at the road for a moment before he began to speak in the same faraway, remembering voice. "We were about your age, I suppose. I remember it was Joe's and my last year at primary school. We always met at the corner where you catch the bus nowadays. Peggy and Joe rode on a big, gentle brute that was half draft horse. Your grandfather used it on the farm in the holidays. There was plenty of room on it for three—I remember sharing it for a while when for some reason or other I was without a horse of my own. But that wouldn't do for young Helen. Oh no, she had to have a pony of her own and because she was the youngest, I suppose, and because she was Helen and liked her own way, your grandfather gave in to her. So there we'd be each morning, a regular procession of us—Joe and Peggy on old Punch, me on tall black Peter and, always in the rear, little Helen on a dapple-gray pony that was almost as headstrong as herself—Puck she called him to match our two P's.

"On this particular day Puck went lame. When I arrived at the corner, your father and your Aunt Peggy were waiting on Punch and there was Helen, a little speck, walking along the road far behind them. I got quite mad with them for not giving her a ride until they explained how they'd tried and tried to get her up on Punch and the pig-headed child had just gone on refusing to be seen riding to school on somebody else's horse. I soon learned what they meant when I went back to meet Helen. I thought she might be too proud to ride three in a row on a great clumsy brute like Punch but would be tickled pink to share my handsome black Peter. Not a hope. She'd got it into her stubborn little head that two on a horse wasn't seemly for Miss Helen Duggan, and when something got into Helen's head, there it stayed.

"So I walked Peter beside her all those four miles to school. What else could I do? She was such a little thing. She must have been about ten, but she looked at least two years younger. She was furious with me and more furious still when I got into trouble for being late. She hated me all day."

"How very unfair!" Tessa was disappointed. She had wanted so much to like the girl who had shared her books,

but it was impossible to like somebody who had hated kind
Mr. Sanderson for keeping her company.

"Next morning," Mr. Sanderson said, smiling, "Puck
was over his lameness. As soon as she saw me, Helen gal-
loped ahead of the others and when she came up to me
jumped off, threw her arms around my leg, which was as
high as she could reach when I was up on Peter, and burst
into tears, she was so ashamed of herself. That was Helen.
And when I saw you striding along the road, so purposeful,
so sure you knew where you were going, I thought, 'That's
Helen's niece,' and that walk to school came back to me.
I hadn't thought of it for years."

Tessa was surprised. Ruth had often said, and Mr. Sanderson had just confirmed, that Aunt Helen was a tiny
person, small and neat and pretty, while she was a long,
thin beanpole like her father. "I've got all Aunt Helen's
books," she said, wondering if reading the same books
could make people alike inside.

Perhaps Mr. Sanderson thought so too because he said,
"Ah, yes, Helen and her books. How she loved them!"

He was not like any other farmer that Tessa knew, but
she liked him. And she remembered that he had been a
lawyer before he inherited Riverlea. He must know all
about the laws. "Mr. Sanderson," she said, "if I found a
calf in the bush . . ."

"You found a calf in the bush?" he asked with flatter-
ing interest.

"I only said *if*." She liked Mr. Sanderson but she could
not share with a stranger a secret that she had kept from
her own father. "Just imagine that I did and suppose she
had no mother and suppose I saved her life, would she
belong to the person who lost the cow? You see, she was
born in the bush and I'm sure the mother died soon after.
That's what I'm pretending," she added quickly.

The laughter wrinkles were deep beside Mr. Sanderson's eyes, but he answered seriously enough, "That's a tricky bit of pretending, Tessa. Are we pretending that the cow was in calf when she wandered into the bush?"

Tessa thought of the honey-gold cow, its coat bright and undamaged. It could not have been in the bush more than a day or two. "I'm sure of it," she said.

"Then I'm afraid, Tessa, that if the imaginary owner of the imaginary cow turned up, the calf would be his property."

"But Cinnamon would have died!"

If Mr. Sanderson had not guessed already, she had given it away now. But he remained stupid, asking questions about the imaginary calf as he might have questioned her about one of her stories. Only the laughter wrinkles hinted at understanding. Tessa was grateful for his feigned stupidity.

"Have you ever been out in the bush at dawn, Mr. Sanderson?" she asked.

Mr. Sanderson looked at her so keenly that she wondered if there were telltale twigs caught in her hair, "Often when I was a boy, Tessa."

"And did Aunt Helen ever go up to the bush at dawn, do you think?"

"I can vouch for it, Tessa. I've seen her there myself."

Tessa sighed with contentment. She had learned two things about Aunt Helen that were not just about the clothes she wore or the kind of washing machine that stood in the kitchen of her apartment. She might have learned more, but before she could think of another question they pulled up at the school gate.

Jenny Wren was just crossing the road to school. She stopped and stared as the blue station wagon pulled up. Then she walked over to the driver's window. Her usually

pale face was quite pink. "Why, Dennis," she said with a
funny little laugh that was almost a giggle, "how good
of you, how very good of you. Don't forget to thank Mr.
Sanderson, Tessa. My dear child, your hair! We'll have to
run a comb through that, won't we, my dear."

Tessa, with the door half open, sat and stared. The
thought of Jenny Wren running a comb through her hair
was as alarming as it was unexpected. And to be Jenny
Wren's dear!

"Come along now, Tessa, we mustn't keep Mr. Sanderson waiting. We know what a busy man he is. Thank you
so much, Dennis, for delivering my stray lamb safely. I'm
sorry that Tessa seems to have lost her tongue, but I'm
sure she's as grateful to you as I am."

Tessa got out of the car and was even more surprised
when Jenny Wren's arm landed on her shoulder and remained there while she waved to the departing station
wagon.

To Tessa's relief Jenny Wren became her normal self as
soon as the station wagon was out of sight. Tessa did not
much care for Jenny Wren's normal self but at least she
knew where she was with it. Her lack of homework was
greeted with all the sarcasm she had expected and her
hair remained uncombed until at lunchtime she dealt with
it herself.

FIVE

The Riverlea Bull

On Friday afternoon Ruth came home from school. Tessa had been so preoccupied with her young animals that she had noted only vaguely the end-of-term fever of the rest of the school. She got the cows in early because she was told to and thought the early milking a piece of good luck because, instead of running out to the bush straight after school and hurrying back again to bring the cows, she could get the milking over and then spend as long as she liked with Cinnamon and Nutmeg. She was taken by surprise when after milking her father said pleasantly, "Coming down to meet the New Plymouth bus with me, Tessa?"

"Oh no, I can't!" she exclaimed in alarm. If she drove with him all the way to town it would be dark when they got back; it would be teatime and she might never escape.

"All right, have it your own way." He held the gate open for her to drive the cows through.

"I can't." It was meant to be an apology but it came out sounding like stubborn disobedience.

"All right, Tessa, we'll leave it at that. Just don't go off with that pup of mine as soon as my back's turned."

But she had to take Sam. Nutmeg expected it. The lie came out angrily, and she really was angry with Dad, who seemed intent on driving her deeper and deeper into deception. "I don't want your silly cattle dog."

Dad's patience snapped. "That's enough, Tessa. I don't know what's come over you lately, but I know I've had enough of your behavior. Do you realize I had to drop

everything and get the truck out yesterday morning because your mother said you'd missed the school bus?"

Nobody had mentioned that before, and although Tessa
knew she should be grateful, their interference annoyed
her. "I was all right," she told him. "Mr. Sanderson gave
me a lift."

"Oh, Mr. Sanderson did, did he?"

She disliked his mocking tone. "And I think you're all
unfair to him. He's the nicest man I've ever met."

"There's no accounting for tastes."

"I wish he was my father." She had not meant to say
that. It was not even true. But once said it was impossible
to take back again. She looked her father steadily in the
eye, as people are supposed to be able to only if they tell
the truth. She did not like what she saw there, but she
lowered her eyes only when his were turned away.

"There's no accounting for tastes," he said again as he
banged the gate shut behind Tessa and the cows.

As she returned along the road after driving the cows to
their paddock, he passed her in the truck. He did not
look at her or wave. She raised her head and forced her
slouching walk into a nonchalant stride. She would not
let him see that she cared.

Yet she had never needed her father more than she did
now. The hopes of yesterday's dawn had been false ones—
if anything, Cinnamon had grown weaker. It took all
Tessa's willpower to enter the little clearing beside the
swimming hole.

As Nutmeg, who had been grazing on her little patch of
grass, ran forward to greet Tessa and the milk, there was
such an air of "And about time too" in her bearing that
Tessa for all her fears could not help smiling.

With Cinnamon it was different. She shuddered as Tessa
knelt down beside her, and although she did not run

away, Tessa could not be sure that it was trust and not
weakness that held her back. Slowly, patiently, Tessa got
her to drink a little milk. But too little. From day to day
she was keeping Cinnamon alive, but was even that a kindness if the calf remained weak and ill for a few days and
then died? Tessa was doing all she knew and it was not
enough. She must tell Dad. Always when she was with
Cinnamon she knew that no anger of his could be as important as the calf's life. And always when she returned home
she failed. She was sure that the world could not contain a
greater coward than Tessa Duggan.

It was dark before she got home, and a drizzle of rain
had begun to fall. The light from the kitchen looked so
inviting that she forgot everything but the comfort it offered. Sam pushed past her as she opened the door, ran
across the floor, leaving a trail of muddy pawmarks, and
jumped on Dad's lap.

"Oh, Tessa, just look at the mess you're making," was
Ruth's greeting after three months' absence. Neither Mum
nor Dad said anything.

They had nearly finished tea. Tessa had scarcely
changed her muddy boots and sat down at the table before
they all moved into the front room, which was seldom
used unless there were visitors. Through two open doors
she could hear Ruth's high voice as she recounted the
gossip of school. Tessa had always dreaded the approach
of her own boarding-school days, but now she envied
Ruth, who came home like a guest and would depart re-
gretted in three weeks' time. Anyone could be pleasant
for three weeks; it was living all year round with people
that was difficult.

Ruth came back into the kitchen with a clean apron
tied around her waist just as Tessa was about to join
the family in the front room.

"Tessa, you weren't going to leave the table just like that?"

Tessa looked at the table and could see nothing wrong with it.

"What about the dishes?"

"Mum didn't tell me to do them."

"If that's the way you've been lately," said Ruth, "I don't wonder Mum and Dad are both fed up with you."

Tessa quietly began to carry the dishes to the sink. As she washed and Ruth dried, Ruth began a new attack. She stood back and viewed Tessa from the tangle of her hair to the long stretch of bare leg at the end of her outgrown and faded jeans. "I suppose that's the sight we've got to put up with all through the holidays," she said.

Tessa took a hand out of the sink and pulled at the frayed wrist of her shirt, leaving a lump of detergent sparkling and bursting its small bubbles. "I don't see why not," she said.

"Well, I'm used to you, of course," said Ruth more kindly, "though I do think it's about time you outgrew this farm-boy business and started looking like a girl. But how's Jan going to like sharing her room with a walking scarecrow?"

"What Jan?" And what was this about sharing a room?

"Jan Freeman, of course. You know she's coming next week."

Tessa had not known, but then so much of her parents' talk had gone unheeded recently while she thought about Nutmeg. Ruth's criticism of her clothes she had heard many times before, but Jan Freeman was Aunt Helen's daughter. "Is Aunt Helen coming too?" she asked eagerly.

"Of course not. She'd hate spending a week on a farm, I bet."

As Tessa turned back, disappointed, to the dishes, the full import of Ruth's words came home to her. She would be expected to share the sunroom with Jan. Ruth's room was so small that the bed already took up more than half the space. Yet when each night Sam was untied from his kennel and settled in a nest of blankets under her mother's sewing table, there was no room for spies in the sunroom. "Jan will have to sleep on the front-room sofa," said Tessa firmly.

"You are growing into a selfish little beast," said Ruth with interest rather than malice.

They finished the dishes in silence.

Next morning Ruth's first words to Tessa when, ravenous after milking, she sat down to breakfast, were "Tessa, you can't come to breakfast with your hair in that state. Can she, Mum?"

Mum looked around from the stove. "It does look a bit as though the birds have been nesting in it, Tessa," she said mildly.

Tessa left the scrambled eggs, the smell of which was making her hunger unbearable, and stamped into the sunroom. Ruth's short fair hair was as sleek as a halo, but she had done nothing except get out of bed and brush it. Farmers like Tessa had half a morning's work to do before breakfast.

But there was worse to come. As Tessa with moderately tidy hair was making for the back door after breakfast, Ruth called to her, "What about the dishes?"

"Well, what about them?" Tessa asked with genuine bewilderment.

"I'm not doing them by myself while you go mooching off across the farm."

Tessa could not say that she had allowed herself to sleep until half past six because there would be all morning to feed Cinnamon and Nutmeg.

"Let the girl go out and help Dad, Ruthie," Mum said, almost pleading with her elder daughter as if it were Ruth and not she who gave the orders. "She's been a little housemaid for weeks and you know how she hates it."

Dad got up from the table and went to the door. "Nobody asks me, of course, whether I want her help."

"Well, do you?" asked Ruth.

"Dunno," said Dad as he pulled on a large boot. "I can manage, I suppose. Got young Colin coming to help me."

Ruth and Tessa looked at each other, and both at the same moment began to giggle. Colin was the fourteen-year-old grandson of their Uncle Alec, a stout, silent boy who had little conversation and only one joke, which was to call them "Auntie Tessa" and "Auntie Ruth" and then to laugh at his own wit with a loud and empty "haw-haw." And it was not even as though they were his real aunts, merely first cousins once removed.

For a moment as they giggled together at Colin and his "Auntie Tessa, haw-haw," it was good to be sisters. Then Ruth returned to the attack.

"There," she said, "Dad doesn't need her, and it'll do her good to help in the house for once. Honest, Mum, she's turning into a real little savage."

Tessa gripped her lip between her teeth to hold back tears that were of anger as much as disappointment. They were all against her.

"If nobody wants me," she said when she had her voice under control, "I'll go for a walk." Time was passing and Cinnamon had still not been fed.

"Oh, Mum," Ruth complained at once, "it isn't fair. Why should I do the dishes by myself?"

"You're not by yourself. You've got Mum to help you."

"Mum's got Daniel to bathe and feed. Mum, can I help bathe him, please? Mum, can I make some scones for Dad's morning tea? And, oh, Mum, we learned the most super recipe for apple dumplings at school and Miss Grant said mine were the best in the class. Can I make some for dinner? Please, Mum."

Mum said yes to everything, as she always did to any reasonable request, which meant that, with a baby to bathe and scones and apple dumplings to make, Ruth was far too busy for housework. She only had time to look up whenever Tessa slackened her pace to suggest another job to be done.

At last it ended. Even Ruth had to agree that somebody must take Dad and Colin their morning tea, and she did not want the job herself.

Ruth was peculiar, Tessa decided as she walked toward Grandpa Pat's house. Here she was with a farm to explore, with calves and baby pigs to visit, and all she wanted to do was stay in the kitchen and make apple dumplings.

But at least to be peculiar was not as bad as being dishonest. And Tessa was shocked by her own dishonesty. With Sam at her side and a bucket of stolen milk in each hand she was going off, with an animal she was forbidden to take, to two animals that she had been keeping secret.

She tied Sam with a piece of twine to the veranda post of Grandpa Pat's house, left the buckets well out of his reach and crossed to the next paddock, where Dad and Colin were cutting scrub.

"Hullo, Auntie Tessa. Haw-haw."

Tessa answered Colin's greeting with no more than a thoughtful stare. He was a big boy, bulging out of jeans that were almost new but already outgrown. Pale-blue, very round eyes in a round pink face gave him an expression of rather melancholy surprise. His dull brown hair was so short that it stood up like the bristles of a worn-down scrubbing brush. "Tea with us?" he asked Tessa, using as always the fewest possible words and speaking slowly in a gruff voice, as if the act of speaking were a difficult job unwillingly performed.

"No, thanks." Tessa was in a panic to be off to the bush with Cinnamon's breakfast.

Colin only grunted, but after many years Tessa could interpret the sounds he used to avoid the labor of speech. The grunt was disappointment. She answered it with a grateful smile. People who were sorry to lose her company seemed rare at present. Almost, if it had not been for Dad's silent and disapproving presence, she would have confided in Colin. He was said to have a way with young and sick animals.

Colin proved useful in another way at dinnertime. Tessa, more worried than ever since her morning visit to Cinnamon, could not cope with the large apple dumpling that Ruth had set before her. It was a beautiful apple dumpling and Ruth was justly proud, but Tessa, who had struggled through the first course with difficulty, felt as if she had eaten a five-course banquet. She politely refused the dumpling and saw Ruth's look of hurt pride. Tessa's farm-boy appetite was a family joke. A pudding so unappetizing that Tessa refused it was a failure indeed.

"P-please," stammered Colin, who had already silently and stolidly plowed through two large helpings of stew and two apple dumplings. "Please, if she don't want it . . ."

Ruth, with a smug look at Tessa, pushed the scorned apple dumpling across the table to him.

As he attacked it like a starving man, there came from the road outside the rattle of a large truck. Noisy brakes brought it to a halt right outside the front gate. Dad jumped to his feet. "That'll be my bull," he said.

Mum and the girls stared at him while Colin attacked his apple dumpling with increased vigor.

"Prompt delivery," Dad went on. He pulled his right-foot boot on his left foot and impatiently tugged it off again. "Young Pat said early afternoon. Reliable fellow, that."

Young Pat. So Dad had bought his Riverlea bull. Tessa looked hopelessly at the pile of dishes on the sink bench which she was beginning to acknowledge as her responsibility. Her disappointment must have been clearly written on her face because Mum said, "Ruth and I'll do the dishes, Tessa. You run along and admire the new bull." And Ruth did not argue.

Joe Duggan's purchase of a Riverlea bull was an event. None of the other local farmers had ever aimed so high. As Tessa followed her father to the truck, Young Pat was leaning out of the cab window talking to a group of men; Uncle Alec was there and his two sons, Ted Howarth and his two biggest boys, and several others.

From the driving seat beside Young Pat, Mr. Sanderson waved to Tessa.

"Bring her along this way, Mr. Sanderson." Dad was full of importance as he guided the truck along the muddy driveway on the far side of the cowyard.

Halfway along the driveway the truck got stuck in the

mud. Young Pat got down from the cab and gave orders
to everyone, his boss included. They had been joined now
by the Hope brothers and Laurie Hope's three children
who had "just happened to be passing," although the
road led only to Uncle Alec's farm. All the men pushed
the truck and laughed and occasionally swore. The children joined in, too, even the little Hope twins, until
Warren Howarth's hand somehow got entangled in Sharon
Hope's hair and her twin sister Patsy thereupon bit him—
hard, Warren said as he pinched Patsy. Gregory Hope
kicked Warren and Billy punched Gregory.

At that moment the truck moved off and they followed
like the best of friends. Without further incident it drew
up at the gate of the paddock that Dad always called the
bull paddock, although it was years since he had kept a
bull of his own.

"But why," asked Mum, who had come out with her
hands still wet from dishwashing, "if it's such a quiet
bull, couldn't you just lead it up the drive?"

She had asked Dad, but Young Pat overheard and
replied for him: "Quiet as a pet lamb, Jean, but sensitive,
being so well bred. He'll be frightened enough by the
journey without being led about in a strange place."

Mum did not sound quite convinced as she said, "I
see."

Several willing men had the paddock gate open. Young
Pat let down the tailboard of the truck, making a ramp
up which he walked importantly, spent a moment inside
and then returned—rather abruptly, Tessa could not help
thinking.

"Scared of a pet lamb, Pat?" asked Bernie Hope, and
the other men laughed.

No bull came and the laughter increased, as if the men

were glad to see Dad's ambitions rewarded with a bull too timid to walk down a ramp. A tractable bull was all very well, but a pedigree animal should have more spirit than to cower in a truck when there was a green paddock spread out before him.

"Better lead him down, Pat," suggested Mr. Sanderson. Young Pat did not move.

"Well, we're here to deliver him, and it doesn't look as though he's planning to deliver himself." Mr. Sanderson stepped onto the ramp and began to climb, quietly and slowly, his hand held out as if in encouragement to a meek pet.

Then he was down again, neither quietly nor slowly, for right behind him was the bull. Mr. Sanderson swerved aside and leaped from the ramp. So did the bull. It headed down the drive.

There was not a man there who had not chased a few bulls in the course of duty. Now it was more in the mood of sport that they snatched up sticks and, brandishing them, fanned out to turn the bull. As it ran with lowered head toward the paddock, Young Pat's voice was full of authority although it came from well in the rear: "Don't panic him. Can't you see the poor beast's frightened!"

When the bull was safely in the paddock Young Pat leaned on the gate beside Mr. Sanderson, who had stayed there ready to shut it behind the bull. "Well, Pat," said Mr. Sanderon, "do you still stand by your guarantee?"

"Guarantee?" asked Young Pat.

"A quiet bull." Mr. Sanderson's voice was also quiet.

"The first bellowing lamb ever raised in Taranaki," said Trevor and then gave a hoot of laughter so loud that the bull on the far side of the paddock looked up and bellowed a reply.

Young Pat slowly turned and leaned his back against the gate. "Nerves, Mr. Sanderson," he explained, "the nerves of a highly strung, highly bred animal. All show to hide his fear, like a person might. Walk into that paddock just quiet like and he'd eat out of your hand."

"Go on, Pat, show us," called several voices,

"Well—er—perhaps not just yet. He wants time to settle in, doesn't he? Just think what he's been through, Mr. Sanderson, shut up in a dark truck, chased by all this crowd. I'm not saying anything about what people do in a moment of panic, mind, but perhaps if he hadn't been rushed at like that, just reasoned with quietly . . ."

"Go in and reason with him, Pat," called Trevor.

"Take him our apologies, Pat," called Bernie Hope.

Trevor pushed past Mr. Sanderson, his hand on the gate, ready to let Young Pat into the paddock. Young Pat sidled away.

It was Dad who came to his rescue. "Who invited you all, anyway?" he asked the men. "Whose bull is it? If I want anybody in there interfering with my livestock, I'll say so. You just get away from that gate, Pat Duggan."

Young Pat, who had been trying to do just that, accepted the invitation.

"You're crazy, Joe," said Trevor as he took his hand away from the catch.

"Think, Joe," said Uncle Alec. "What use is a bull you can't control on a farm this size with fences in the state yours are in?" He held up the rusty end of the fence of the bull's own paddock. "Don't be a fool, man, when the Hope boys can let you have a fine biddable animal at half the price."

"I got a Riverlea bull, haven't I?" Dad was as stubborn as a spoiled child with his heart set on a toy. "Can I help it if you guys are jealous? Now just get out and give him a chance to settle down without all of you treating him like a circus."

"That's the style, Joe," said Young Pat. "You heard him, men. It's his own land he's ordering you off."

"Fun's over, boys," growled Uncle Alec and led the way back toward the road.

The bull began to graze at the far side of the paddock. It was a beautiful animal with a powerful head and shoulders and long, slim flanks, richly dark for a Jersey and so sleek that it glowed like a ruby in the sunlight. Though grazing, it was not at rest. From time to time the muscular neck was raised and two small eyes looked at the little group beside the gate with an expression that was neither mild nor friendly.

Dad, having rid himself of his uninvited visitors, gazed and gazed with the unaccustomed dreaminess in his eyes that Tessa had seen more than once since Daniel was born.

Mr. Sanderson spoke twice before he was heard. "Well, Joe," he said, "are you satisfied with your bargain?"

"Too right," said Dad without taking his eyes from the bull.

"And if your little girl can't go in there and stroke his nose tomorrow morning," said Young Pat, "my name's not Pat Duggan."

"She'll do no such thing," said Mum. Her alarm was unnecessary because Tessa was sure she would never dare. Dad said the bull was safe, Young Pat guaranteed it, but there was a look in the bright little eyes that warned against any experiment in nose stroking.

As they walked back along the drive she asked Colin what he thought.

"Uncle Joe says he's okay," he told her almost reproachfully.

Tessa was ashamed. If Colin could trust Dad's judgment, she should be able to do the same. She resolved to believe in the quietness of the Riverlea bull as long as she was not asked to put it to the test by stroking its nose.

SIX

Colin

When Tessa went to get the cows next morning she was not surprised to see that the pigs had broken into the cow paddock. The fence between the pigsty and the cow paddock had been for some time badly in need of repair. She was walking across the paddock before she saw that the pigs were not in fact the real culprits. At the far end, at some distance from the pigs, stood the Riverlea bull. She backed hastily to the gate, shut it and leaned against it.

At some time during the night the bull must have broken first into the pigstye and then out the other side into the cow paddock. It was not the action of a mild-mannered animal.

Tessa had read about people being chased by bulls, but, until Mr. Sanderson's swift descent of the ramp, she had never seen such a thing in real life. And she lived in dairying country. What would her father say if she returned to tell him that she was frightened of an animal that was supposed to be as quiet as a pet lamb?

She pushed down the voice inside her that said that pet lambs do not break through fences, and again opened the gate. Only two cows were waiting there today; the rest, although they seemed to have recovered from the excitement of the bull's arrival, were scattered about the paddock. Tessa went boldly forward to round them up. She kept her eyes from the bull. To watch a feared object only breeds new and imaginary fears.

She was driving the cows toward the gate, alongside the electric fence that divided the paddock into two, when the pounding of hooves across the grass made her look back. The bull was charging toward her with low-ered head. Quickly she rolled under the electric fence. The bull pulled up short, digging a skid mark a yard long in the muddy ground.

She began to walk toward the gate and the bull on his side of the fence kept pace with her. The gate was open, and she was leading him straight toward it!

She stopped dead. So did the bull. At least if she could keep him there until Dad came to see why she was so long in bringing the cows. . . . But she wished the single strand of the electric fence did not look so thin. Suppose there was a sudden power failure and suppose the bull knew the meaning when the steady "tock tock" of the fence stopped. Suppose he took a leap at it and jumped it. It was not very high.

"Hello, Auntie Tessa!" Tessa would never have be-lieved that she could be so thankful to hear Colin's feeble joke.

"Colin, shut the gate!" she screamed a moment later as the bull turned to face the new intruder. She could see under the shining coat his thick muscles gathering them-selves for a rush that would take him not only toward Colin but to the road and escape.

Colin slammed the gate shut and disappeared. A mo-ment later he was back again, astride the gate with a stout fence post in his hand. Without a word he sat there as Tessa and the bull, with the electric fence between them, walked side by side down the paddock. They had nearly reached him before he spoke. "Run when I say," he said.

You could not argue with a person who spoke so little.

Tessa stood watching him. So did the bull, with growing interest, as he hauled himself down from the gate and advanced toward it with the heavy fence post raised in both hands.

"Now, run for it!" he shouted when he was almost against the bull's nose.

Tessa rolled under the fence and ran as she had never run before. As she leaned on the road side of the gate, Colin, very slowly, with his fence post still raised, backed away. Almost at the gate he turned and ran, dropped the fence post and hauled himself across. The bull's breath must have warmed the seat of his jeans as it lunged, snorting, after him.

Colin silently picked up his bicycle from the roadside and pushed it along as they drove the cows down the road. The bull leaned its head over the gate and bellowed.

"I could hit the man who ruined that bull," said Colin.

Tessa stared at him. She had pitied herself, been terrified for Colin, but she had not thought of pitying the bull.

"Stands to reason," Colin went on. "He's against people, but he's terrified of a man with a stick. Ruined, that's what, a beautiful animal like that."

Dad was waiting in the cowyard. He listened to their story, which Tessa told since Colin, after an outburst that was long for him, had retreated into his normal silence.

"You'd better be right," he told Colin as he grasped a pitchfork that was leaning against the wall of the cowstall. "And if you are, when I've finished with Dennis Sanderson he's going to regret the day he was born." He spoke so fiercely that Tessa was not sure whether the pitchfork was for Mr. Sanderson or the bull.

She watched in safety from behind the cowyard gate

until the bull came trotting along the road, with Dad and Colin behind him. The youngest calf on the farm could not have looked more docile.

"Perhaps I was silly," she suggested when the bull was locked inside the most solidly built of the farm sheds and they were busy with the milking. Colin, who had been on his way to spend a Sunday with his grandfather, stayed to help. They were running late.

"You wasn't silly," he said. "I seen the look on that bull's face. Wanted to make mincemeat of you. What you going to do with him now, Uncle Joe?"

"You'll see," Dad muttered, looking down into a bucket of milk with an expression fit to curdle it.

Colin was ordered rather than invited to stay for breakfast, and after the meal he and Tessa were pushed into the little Ford truck and driven off toward Riverlea. "You're my witnesses," Dad told them. "Mr. Lawyer Sanderson will want witnesses, no doubt."

Tessa felt Colin, crammed in beside her, squirm uncomfortably. She felt uncomfortable too. She hated to see her father lose control of his temper—it turned him into something so much less than the father she knew. Now, while he kept silent, she could see his face pulled tightly together as if its muscles held down his anger like a cork in a bottle. She knew how that cork would shoot out as he began to talk to Mr. Sanderson and the anger would burst free in words that he did not mean.

Mr. Sanderson didn't help. He had just got home from eight o'clock Communion and stepped out of the garage to meet them, neat and gray-suited in contrast to a man whose Sunday morning was spent working and who might occasionally get to church at eleven if sufficiently bullied by his wife.

"Rescuing my daughter from your savage bull," was

how he described his morning's activities, which was
hardly fair to Colin, who had done any rescuing that
was needed.

Mr. Sanderson looked at Tessa with concern. "You
weren't hurt?" he asked.

"Isn't your fault or your bull's that she wasn't killed."

"Let the child tell her own story, Joe," said Mr. Sanderson.

Tessa told her story, making the most of Colin's rescue.

"That was very courageous," said Mr. Sanderson, looking with interest at Colin's clumsy bulk.

Colin went red and rubbed the foot of one boot vio-
lently up and down the leg of the other. "Stands to reason," he said. "Saw it yesterday."

"Pity you didn't say so at the time." Dad's anger
swerved across to Colin, then returned to its first target.
"Pity somebody else don't know as much about his own
livestock as a kid of fourteen."

"I might say the same about the man who bought the
livestock, Joe."

"Oh, yeah, typical lawyer's talk that is. Turn the whole
thing around and put the other fellow in the wrong. You
just listen here, Dennis Sanderson. I got half the men in
the district to witness you guaranteed that bull as quiet as
a lamb."

"Now hold on, Joe. Did I say the bull was quiet?"

"Oh, yes, you just play the big boss and let Young Pat
take the blame. That's nice, that is, from a man fresh
out of church. A nice Christian attitude, sneaking out
of your responsibilities and putting the blame on someone else."

There was a flash of anger across Mr. Sanderson's
face before he calmly replied: "Man alive, do you imagine I'm delighted to hear that your little girl's been

chased by a bull? But we won't get anywhere by standing here calling each other names. Young Pat's the one that knows about the bull. Just come down to the milking shed and see what he's got to say for himself. He can give the explanation. I admit that the responsibility's mine. Satisfied?"

Dad shrugged his shoulders. He wanted a fight and he was not getting one. The bottled-up anger was held down with difficulty as he slouched behind Mr. Sanderson toward the milking shed.

Young Pat had just begun milking. Tessa wondered whether it was the aristocracy of the Riverlea cows or Young Pat's preference that allowed them to keep such late hours.

He looked up to smile a welcome to his visitors. "How's the bull coming along, Joe?" he asked. "Settling in nicely?"

"Shouldn't you be asking how many of my family it's put in the hospital?"

The milking-machine cups clattered from Young Pat's hand onto the concrete floor. "Oh, no!" he said.

"You don't seem very surprised at your pet lamb's misdeeds," said Mr. Sanderson.

"Look, Mr. Sanderson, I'm new here, aren't I. Can't know all about every animal on the place yet, can I?"

"Then you shouldn't give guarantees about every animal on the place."

"Look, Mr. Sanderson, Ted Howarth's been doing odd jobs about the place for your brother for years. Ted's had the handling of that bull since it was born. He said . . ."

"Let's go and see Ted Howarth." Dad was off at once along the drive.

"Hold on, Joe," called Mr. Sanderson. "This is Riverlea

business. And that means Pat's business and mine. We employ Howarth to help out sometimes, but that's our responsibility. We guaranteed you a quiet bull and we face the music. Isn't that so, Pat?"

Young Pat, rather uncertainly, smiled his agreement.

"You youngsters," said Mr. Sanderson to Colin and Tessa, who were both listening with interest, "have you ever looked over the Riverlea garden? No? Oh, but you should. My sister-in-law had a real showplace here."

Neither of them cared half so much for a garden as for the outcome of the bull episode, but they knew when they were not wanted.

The garden was laid out on a hillside above the river and there was art in the way Mrs. Sanderson had guided it from formality around the homestead at the top to merge with the untamed bush at the foot of the hill. Tessa was enchanted by the swathes of daffodils holding up stiff buds, the wide lawns, and the rock garden that sprawled down the steepest slope with a little waterfall and pools. She had never imagined that a garden could be so big or so magnificent.

It was a long time before Dad called down to them from the veranda of the big house. Mr. Sanderson stood beside him, but not Young Pat.

"Well, that's it, Joe," Mr. Sanderson was saying as Tessa hurried up, breathless from the climb. "Pat and I will be over in about an hour to collect him. No hard feelings then, Joe?" He held out his hand.

Dad looked at the hand and seemed to hesitate before he took it briefly in his own. "And you'll get those repairs done straight away?" he asked distrustfully. "Can't have the pigs running about loose, and that brute of yours has done a fair bit of damage to the sty."

"I'll send Pat and Ted over first thing tomorrow."

On the way home Tessa tried to find out more about what had been said, but Dad's temper had gone into its sulky phase, as it always did when people wouldn't let him flare up and get it out of his system. She could get little more from him than grunts.

Colin decided to postpone his visit to his grandfather so that he could "see the fun," as he put it, when Mr. Sanderson and Young Pat came for the bull. Tessa supposed that he went to the cowyard with Dad, or perhaps to check that the bull was secure. She was not interested in them, for she had only one thought in her head—in all the morning's excitement she had not yet fed Cinnamon.

She was hurrying past Grandpa Pat's house with Sam when, in the next paddock, walking along with his hands in his pockets as though he had nowhere in particular to go and all day to get there, she saw Colin. His back was to her and she might have got safely past him if Sam had not bounded toward him with joyful barks. Colin turned to see where he had come from and looked straight at Tessa with a bucket of milk in each hand and a bright-red face.

"Hello, Auntie Tessa!" He paused a moment to pat Sam and then walked on.

Her secret was safe and yet, from gratitude perhaps, or the weight of a long loneliness, she stopped and called to him, "Don't you want to know where I'm going?"

"Your own business."

"Wouldn't you like to see?"

"If you want to show me."

Friendship with Colin was hard work. She could not tell as they walked toward the bush whether he was interested or just polite. But she knew that she was glad not to be going to the swimming hole alone. Colin understood animals. He had understood the Riverlea bull better than any of the men, even Dad.

She made her confidence in silence, as he might himself, by leading him to the clearing beside the swimming hole where Cinnamon still lay on a nest of ferns that Tessa had made for her the night before. Dull eyes that seemed almost to fill the skeleton-thin face looked up at the intruders.

Nutmeg came bouncing across the clearing, but Colin seemed not to notice her. When he looked at Tessa his round eyes were full of reproach. "She's starving," he said.

Tessa silently handed him the bucket. She felt as guilty as if she had been trying to starve Cinnamon, instead of spending hour after heartbreaking hour providing the little food that had kept her alive.

She watched closely as he fed the calf. She could not see that he did anything that she had not tried already. The only difference was that he succeeded where time after time she had failed. He did not get Cinnamon to drink all the milk but he did better than Tessa ever had.

"She's cold," he said when it was plain that Cinnamon would drink no more.

"I've done my best."

Colin looked his thoughts about her best. "Reckon I can carry her home," he said. "Skinny little thing," he added as if calling Cinnamon by a pet name.

"No, Colin, please." Tessa poured out her story. It was a relief to be telling somebody at last. "And this morning when he's in a bad mood already!" she added. "He'll be furious!"

"Got to keep her warm," said Colin, and Tessa knew that her troubles could never be as real to Colin as those of an animal in need.

"Couldn't we . . ." Tessa paused in the middle of the sentence, wondering how it would end. "Couldn't we take her to Grandpa Pat's house?"

Colin thought that over. "Don't see why not," he said at last. "Only, look, Tessa, two feeds a day aren't no good to a sick baby calf. I reckon she'll need feeding every couple of hours or so."

"But the other calves . . ."

"The other calves aren't sick. Look, Tessa, she can't take more 'n a little bit at a time, so you give her a lot of little feeds. Stands to reason."

"I see," said Tessa. It seemed so obvious now that she couldn't think why she had failed to see it for herself.

"Reckon Uncle Joe oughter to be told," said Colin in the uncertain voice of the nearly defeated.

"Please, Colin."

Colin muttered that he supposed, maybe, he didn't know. And then he gently lifted the frail creature and led the way to Grandpa Pat's house. As he walked he spoke softly to her—words that, when Tessa caught a few of them, seemed to be in a language of his own. Or perhaps Cinnamon's too, for the feeble complaints with which she had begun the journey were soon forgotten and she snuggled her nose under Colin's arm.

They made her as comfortable as they could on the veranda of the old house with Ruth's ruined cushion behind her to keep off the drafts. Colin promised to take some bales of straw from the cowyard as soon as his uncle's back was turned. "We're bein' awful dishonest," he said.

"To save an animal," said Tessa promptly. She was beginning to understand Colin. Anything that would help an animal must be done at any cost; anything that hurt an animal must be avoided like the plague.

They arrived back at the farm buildings as Young Pat and Ted Howarth, both armed with pitchforks, were steering a very meek Riverlea bull into Mr. Sanderson's cattle truck.

"Sorry about that, Joe," said Mr. Sanderson when the door was safely fastened behind it. "I hear the Hope boys have a young bull with Riverlea blood . . ."

"I'll find my own bull, thanks," Dad interrupted. As the truck moved off he stood looking after it as though he could see through its sides the Riverlea bull with its proud head and ruby coat. He was still watching long after the truck was out of sight.

"Isn't no time for telling him things," Colin whispered. "Better get the straw."

Tessa ran joyfully ahead of him to the shed where the straw was kept. She trusted Colin and her trust made her silly with happiness. She danced with a heavy bale of straw all the way to Grandpa Pat's house, keeping up a stream of unnatural chatter and silly jokes at which Colin did not laugh. She didn't mind his seriousness. Colin was all right.

SEVEN

Jan

Tessa did not want to go to town to meet her cousin Jan. Jan was Ruth's visitor. But Ruth was so busy polishing floors and arranging vases of daffodils that she had no time to meet the guest for whom those preparations were being made. And Dad flatly refused to go alone.

So Tessa sat beside her father in the old truck and thought that Jan was a nuisance and that Ruth was even more of one. She was too tired to meet strange cousins. Since Colin began to help with Cinnamon she had slept in her own bed only every other night.

Colin, when he gave himself a job to do, did it thoroughly. When Tessa hurried down to Grandpa Pat's house on Monday morning with Cinnamon's breakfast she had found him there in his sleeping bag inside a mound of straw with an alarm clock beside his ear. "Two-hourly feedings," he had calmly explained when the clock jangled him awake.

Tessa was ashamed. Her twice-daily feedings of Cinnamon seemed like neglect. She was grateful to Colin when he allowed her to take that night's vigil.

It had been a night of terror, that first night at Grandpa Pat's. Although she had taken Sam for company, the loneliness of the old house among the moonlit hills had been almost too much for her. Moreporks hooted from the bush, possums scrambled across the roof, and the house creaked and groaned as it never did by day. After half an hour she ran for home.

She crawled, shivering, into her own bed and hid her

head under the bedclothes. But she could not sleep. Long after she was warm again she lay awake in shame. At last, less willingly than she had ever moved in her life, she made her way back to Grandpa Pat's house. She stayed there for the rest of the night and, with her arms tightly clasped around Sam, even slept a little between the two-hourly calls of the alarm clock.

It was not until this morning, after her third night at the old house, that her reward had come. When she woke in the dawn light, Cinnamon was standing beside her, legs splayed out and shaky, but no fear in her eyes and with her nose thrust down to sniff at Tessa's face with the curiosity of reviving health. And Colin, when he called in before he began the day's work for his uncle, said he had never seen such a change in a sick animal.

With the image of the healthy calf still clear in her mind, Tessa leaned back against the seat of the jolting truck and closed her eyes in weary contentment. The battle was won. Cinnamon would live. Colin said so and she had learned to trust Colin.

"I'll never recognize her," muttered Dad in a misery of shyness. "If the girl has to have visitors, why can't she . . ."

"I think," said Tessa, opening her eyes as she concentrated on the more immediate problem, "that she must be an odd sort of girl if she's going to be upset unless the house is full of flowers and all polished up."

Dad grinned at her. "Another little Ruthie, eh, old son?"

Tessa giggled until the tears ran down her face. Dad had called her "old son" for the first time since Daniel was born. He smiled across the steering wheel at the road ahead as if content that he had pleased her.

They did not speak again but they were cozily aware of their old friendship for the rest of the journey to town.

Only half a dozen people got off the New Plymouth

bus and of those only one was a young girl traveling alone. As they shuffled toward her the girl ran forward, smiling and waving. She was only a little thing, no taller than Tessa and just as thin, but where Tessa at twelve was a tall person on the way up, all loose arms and legs, Jan at fifteen was a neat little person who was meant to be small.

"You're Uncle Joe," she said, holding out her hand. "Helen's talked of you so often. And this must be Tessa." She looked around, as if surprised by the absence of Ruth.

Tessa and her father reached out to take Jan's suitcase and their long arms tangled together like snakes. Tessa quickly withdrew hers. She had done the wrong thing. Ruth had done the wrong thing in not meeting her own visitor, and Jan, who was so grown up that she called her mother "Helen," was on the point of despising the whole family.

"I'll get in the back," Tessa offered as they reached the truck. She often squeezed in the front with Mum or Ruth, but she was sure that Jan had never been asked before to cram with two other people into the front of an elderly truck.

"You'll do no such thing," said Dad, as alarmed as if she had suggested leaving him in the cab with a wild animal.

"Surely there's room for three skinny people like us," said Jan. It was a silly word for Jan to use about herself. Tessa and her father were skinny; Jan was slim. But Tessa was too shy to say so. She got silently into the truck between her father and Jan.

Jan talked all the way home. At first both Dad and Tessa answered as briefly as they could when they were asked a direct question. And there were plenty of questions. Jan was interested in everything—the family, the whole Manurima district. And somehow by the end of the journey Dad was explaining the working of the farm to her as easily as if he had been talking to another farmer. But Tessa remained silent and nervous. If anything, Jan's ease at talking to a strange adult made her more foreign and frightening than ever.

There was no shyness in either Mum or Ruth. They came down the path in a flood of welcome and swept Jan into the house. Tessa, her own part done, retreated to Grandpa Pat's house and the company of Cinnamon. She stayed there until milking time.

Bedtime came and Tessa and Jan were alone in the sunroom. While Tessa undressed, Jan knelt beside the bookcase and began to read the titles of the books. "You've got some lovely books here, Tessa," she said.

Tessa went hot all over and got herself entangled in the shirt she was trying to pull over her head. Years ago, when she was just beginning to read, Uncle Alec had found the books, damp and moldy, lying in a shed behind his house, which had been in the family home when Aunt Helen was a girl. He had given them to Tessa and she had made them her own through years of loving and rereading. But they belonged to Aunt Helen and Jan as surely as Cinnamon belonged to some unknown farmer who had lost a honey-gold cow. None of the things that felt like her dearest possessions were really hers, not the books, nor Cinnamon, nor Sam. Even Nutmeg, now she was weaned, became each day more like a wild creature who belonged to herself.

"Such a nice old-fashioned lot. You're not a haunter of secondhand bookshops, are you, Tessa?"

Tessa shook her head, shirt and all. It was only from books that she had learned that such places existed.

"Were they your mother's?" Jan sounded doubtful. Even for someone who had known her only a day it was difficult to imagine Mum as a bookworm. "You know, there are books here I've only heard about from Helen talking about what she read when she was young. I wish she were here. She'd be thrilled."

Tessa extricated herself from her shirt to see Jan flicking over the pages of a book. Sooner or later she must come to the flyleaf where, as in all the books, Helen Duggan's name was clearly written.

"They're her books. They're all your mother's except those paperbacks on the top shelf."

Jan turned to the front of the book and looked in silence at the girlish writing.

"So really they're yours," Tessa gabbled in a fever of guilt. "I didn't think anyone wanted them and you were in England then, anyway, but they're yours really. I've taken care of them, honestly. I found this old bookcase and mended it and painted it myself. I never thought of it being stealing until now. And I'm giving them back."

Jan smiled up at her. "I don't think," she said, "I've ever been offered such a wonderful present."

Tessa, taking Jan's gratitude for acceptance, turned from hot to shivery cold. "But they're not a present. They're yours by rights. Though I suppose you're too old for most of them now."

While Jan was washing up, Tessa, unable to resist a book, had flicked through the one that lay on the table at Jan's bedside. It seemed to have a lot of love and very little adventure, a combination quite the opposite of anything in the bookcase and of Tessa's own tastes.

Jan was talking and Tessa did not at once bother to listen. ". . . and of course they're yours. You rescued them and loved them. I know Helen would agree." There was a long pause between hearing the words and finally taking in their meaning. And then another pause while Tessa found they meant something even more important.

"Jan!" All shyness was gone. "Jan, what you said, rescuing and loving. Would Aunt Helen really say that—about anything?"

"She'd love you to keep the books."

"Mr. Sanderson said . . . Oh, never mind." How could a town girl understand about Cinnamon?

Jan looked ready to embark on more of her questions, but before she could speak Sam began to howl from the kennel to which he had been chained for the first time at night. "That poor little pup," said Jan. "He sounds as if his little heart will break."

Tessa said nothing. If Sam's heart broke it was Jan's own fault for trespassing in another person's sunroom.

"Tessa, couldn't we . . ." Jan's brown eyes sparkled. "Oh, but Tessa, you do!" Her eyes, darting like flames as they surveyed the room, had caught and interpreted the old blanket mottled with black and white hairs that had been carelessly pushed under Tessa's bed.

As Jan hurried out to fetch Sam, Tessa dragged out the blanket and shook it into the loose folds that Sam liked. She was grateful to Jan—she had two very good reasons to be grateful—but when Jan returned with Sam in her arms she crouched under the sewing table with her arms full of blanket, imprisoned by shyness.

When Tessa came in from the farm next morning to get the men's morning tea Mum and Ruth were preparing Daniel's bath. Jan sat in Dad's high-backed chair in the corner watching them.

She jumped up with alarming eagerness when Tessa picked up the basket and canteen. "Can I come too?" she asked.

Tessa looked appealingly at Mum and Ruth. Because she shared her sunroom with Ruth's visitor it did not mean that she had to have Jan tagging along with her all day as well.

"Oh, Jan," said Ruth, disappointed, "you can't go now. He's so sweet in his bath. And if you watch this once, Mum might let you help another time. But she has to watch first, like I did, doesn't she, Mum?"

"Now, Ruthie," said Mum, "perhaps Jan isn't interested in bathing babies."

Jan smiled at her. "It's such a pity to be inside on a morning like this. Why don't you come with us, Ruth? I'm sure Auntie Jean can manage without you just this once."

Ruth looked unhappily from her visitor to her brother and then back again. "You can't go in those shoes anyway," she said. "You don't know how muddy it is out there. It's awful."

Jan, undismayed, borrowed a pair of Ruth's outgrown boots, which were awkwardly large and threatened to come off at every step. But she seemed happy as she stumbled across the paddocks carrying the basket with the food and mugs. To Tessa's alarm she talked about how she was simply dying to see Grandpa Pat's house, of which Helen had told her so much. "You can die then," Tessa mentally told her.

"Hello, Auntie Jan." Tessa could have shaken Colin for the fool he made of himself as he stood round-eyed and openmouthed staring at Jan. Suddenly he burst into a wave of high-pitched laughter, quite different from his usual gruff "haw-haw," and his face grew redder and redder. Just as Tessa was wondering if he would laugh himself into some kind of fit, he stopped and said, "You are my auntie, isn't she, Auntie Tessa?" Then he grabbed a sweet bun and stuffed it into his mouth as if trying to gag himself.

"How can Ruth bear it?" Jan said on their way home. "To live on a farm and stick inside all day when there must be so many exciting things to do!"

Tessa agreed with her, but she was not going to say so. Ruth's tastes were no concern of a stranger-cousin.

She was thankful to see that after lunch Ruth and her visitor settled down together in the sunroom, Ruth at the sewing machine and Jan with her book. They did not look very companionable, but at least they were together and it would not be fair either to Ruth or Tessa if Jan followed her about the farm all the time. Yet somehow she felt a little selfish as she sat on the veranda of Grandpa Pat's house, which Jan had so much wanted to see.

"Like me to stay with her tonight?" asked Colin when he joined her there after the day's work.

"Of course not. I'll get out somehow. That wretched Jan!"

Colin looked at her with round, hurt eyes. "She isn't wretched."

"You don't have to share your bedroom with her."

Colin blushed to the roots of his stubbly hair. Tessa was almost certain that she could see his scalp blushing through the hair itself. "You got a crush on her or something?" she asked.

Colin's pale-blue eyes seemed to stand out like a fish's in a face that was almost purple with blushing. "She's so . . . so . . ." he stammered. "Look, Tessa, I wish Uncle Joe hadn't got rid of that old bull. I wish he could chase her and I could be walkin' past and—why did it have to be only you? Only that weren't really brave. No, she'd be right in the paddock with him, see, and I'd pick her up and carry her out of his path and she'd be safe but I'd be there protecting her and he'd turn on me and kill me. But she'd remember me for always."

It was the longest speech Tessa had ever heard Colin make. She considered it seriously. "If he was so fierce, wouldn't he turn on her when you were dead?" she asked.

Colin thought that over. "I know what," he said at last. "I've got her over the fence, see, but before I can get over myself along comes the old bull and slash, borump, there I am dead on the ground at her feet and the old bull prancing about with blood all over his horns." Colin paused for a moment as if relishing the bloodthirsty scene. Then, in his normal voice, he said, "Maybe if we have to do a story in English next term, I'll write that. Gosh, Tessa, it's a real story like in a book. Tessa, what can I do when there isn't no bull?"

With difficulty she directed his attention back to Cinnamon and the question of her attendant for the night. By keeping Jan's name out of it, she succeeded in getting him to agree that, since he had been on duty last night, she would take tonight's turn as usual. But there was still a glazed, fishlike look in his eyes when they parted to go home to tea.

Jan's book was apparently an absorbing story and Jan was near the end. That night in bed she read on and on. Several times she suggested that Tessa should turn out her light, but Tessa silently went on with her own book, although the concentration needed to keep her eyes open left her little to spare for taking in what she read.

At last, with a sigh in which Tessa recognized the combination of satisfaction and loss that she had often felt herself at the end of a good book, like a parting of old friends, Jan laid down her book and switched off her bedhead light.

Tessa did the same and waited in the darkness, staring at a beam of starlight between the curtains to keep herself awake until she thought she had given Jan time to fall asleep. Jan was so curious that she was sure that if she were awake she would have asked questions as she dressed in her warmest clothes, roused Sam, and crept through the outside door.

It was her fourth night at the old house and so thoroughly had custom and gathering tiredness destroyed her early fears that, forgetting to set the alarm after Cinnamon's four-o'clock feed, she was only awakened by the morning sun when it shone directly on her face. The alarm clock pointed to a minute past seven.

She hastily gave Cinnamon her overdue feed and ran all the way to the cowyard. The cows were already in and being milked. Dad looked up from where he was tying a leg rope on Daisy. "Well, sleepyhead," he called to her heartily, "just as well we've got one early riser in the family." Far from being angry as she had expected, he seemed in a particularly good mood.

Tessa went into the little room off the cowstalls where she could hear the separator chugging, expecting to see Colin, even perhaps Ruth suddenly turned farm girl. The last person she could have imagined there was Jan, her hair tousled as if she had slipped out of bed without combing it, her shirt streaked gray and brown with mud and a wet brown patch on the seat of her jeans where she had sat down in the mud. It probably happened on the treacherous spot at the cow paddock gate, guessed Tessa, who had more than once come to grief there herself.

Jan laughed gaily as Tessa mentioned her guess. She seemed a different person from the bored girl who had lounged about the house yesterday. "Doesn't it make you feel important?" she asked.

Tessa stared at her, not understanding.

"I suppose it's all in the day's work to you. You wouldn't understand what it's like for—a townee, isn't that what you call us?—to get up early in the morning and . . . Tessa, I was terrified of the cows. They looked so big and I didn't think for a moment they'd let me order them about. But they did—except for one."

"Daisy," laughed Tessa.

"Tessa," said Jan, lowering her voice to a whisper, "Uncle Joe thinks you overslept."

"So I did."

"In the sunroom, I mean. That's the impression I left with him without telling a downright lie."

"Thanks," said Tessa and waited for the battery of questions she had learned to expect from Jan.

But Jan asked no questions, not even when they were alone visiting the calves and pigs before breakfast. She seemed interested in nothing except the young animals, laughing like a little girl at the mock battles of the calves or at the old sow lying on her side with a dozen pink piglets lined up for breakfast.

By the time they had finished their own breakfast Tessa had made up her mind. She followed Jan into the sunroom and watched her make her bed.

"Jan," she said nervously, "did you know I was out all night?"

Jan shook up her pillow and laid it over the neatly folded sheet. "I heard you go out," she said.

"Don't you want to know why?"

"Only if you want to tell me."

"But I do, please." Tessa could not have explained why. Perhaps because Jan, who asked so many questions, had not asked this one; perhaps because Jan had almost lied for her sake; or perhaps because it would be easy to tell Jan.

Jan sat down on her half-made bed and listened to Tessa's account of her meeting with the cow, the kid, and the calf. She did not interrupt until Tessa reached Colin's part of the story. "What, that half-witted boy who works for your father?" she asked.

"He isn't half-witted!" cried Tessa, blushing for Colin almost as he might have blushed for himself.

"He seemed most peculiar to me."

"That's because . . ." But Tessa realized in time that Colin's feelings about Jan were something that Jan must never know. "He's wonderful with animals. And he rescued me from a ferocious bull." She told Jan the story of the Riverlea bull, dwelling with enthusiasm on Colin's heroic advance with the fence post.

Jan was only moderately impressed. Colin might be a heroic half-wit but he remained half-witted, and brains, Tessa gathered, were more important to her than physical courage. Poor Colin. He might die a hundred deaths to rescue Jan, but he could never make himself clever.

When the bedspread was neatly on Jan's bed and Tessa's had received its usual brusque treatment, they went together to visit Cinnamon. Neither suggested it, but it seemed the natural thing to do when Jan had been told the story.

Colin was already at Grandpa Pat's house, feeding Cinnamon. Jan watched with interest as the calf, with a confidence now that was almost greed, emptied the bucket.

"Is she very weak still?" she asked.

Colin looked up at her and blushed, then down into the bucket and thought. "She's doin' awright," he said at last. "Gonner tell Tessa we can give up the night feeds now."

"But she looks so unhappy." It was true. Cinnamon, her meal over, stood beside Colin with her head hanging down and her big eyes dim and sad. She was not the skeleton-thin creature of a week ago. Colin and Tessa could see her improvement. But when Tessa tried to look at her as Jan must, seeing the calf for the first time, she had to admit that Cinnamon was a thin, dull-coated creature with no sign of a young animal's zest for life.

"The calves we saw this morning," Jan went on, "were so full of bounce and crazy games. Isn't that the way young animals should be?"

"Tha's a fact," said Colin slowly. "Reckon she could be lonely. Reckon she might be happier in the calf paddock now." He looked reproachfully at Tessa.

Jan looked at Tessa too, but as if, Tessa uncomfortably thought, she was trying to read her mind. "That would mean telling Uncle Joe," she said, "and Tessa doesn't want that. I'm just an ignorant townee, Colin, but if she needs a friend, couldn't we catch the little goat? Weren't they friends?"

Colin and Tessa looked at each other and their eyes signaled that Jan was a wonderful and clever person. "Could be missing her little cobber at that," said Colin, and without another word he set out toward the bush. The two girls had to run to catch up with him.

They found Nutmeg in her old place beside the swimming hole, standing at the water's edge with her head bowed as if she watched her own reflection and found it poor company.

"What d'you call her?" asked Colin.

Tessa told him.

Colin walked slowly toward the kid. "Nutty, Nutty, come on, little Nutcase." Nutmeg waited until his hand was almost touching her, then backed away, but she did not turn and run as she had run from her old friend, Tessa, more than once in the past week. "Old Nutcase, eh," said Colin as if it were a private joke between them. Nutmeg certainly treated it like one. She circled him with skips and jumps that were positively flirtatious, daintily accepted a bunch of leaves from his hand and at last, when he moved away, still calling her by his insulting nicknames, she followed him, bleating her distress at his desertion. Like all Colin's dealings with animals, it looked absurdly simple, but to Tessa, who had tried to persuade Nutmeg to leave the bush and failed, it was little short of magic. She could not help feeling jealous of Colin, who had so easily won her friend's devotion, as he led Nutmeg, as if by an invisible halter, out of the bush and to Grandpa Pat's house.

There was no doubt that the two young animals remembered each other. For Nutmeg the reunion was a gay occasion, but Cinnamon still had the sobriety of an invalid. She sniffed at Nutmeg's nose whenever Nutmeg's gleeful buck-jumping left it still enough to be sniffed, but at first she seemed content to be an audience.

Then a wonderful thing happened. As Nutmeg approached her with one of her stiff-legged jumps, Cinnamon, who had never before undertaken any exercise more lively than a slow plod along the veranda, leaped in imitation. Nutmeg sprang up on Ruth's chair and stood looking down at her friend with her head on one side. Cinnamon hesitated a moment and then, putting her front feet on the chair, reached up and touched the nose of the kid with her own. Sam, who apparently thought he had

been left out of things long enough, circled the chair, yapping. At once Nutmeg leaped down in pursuit and Cinnamon, head lowered in imitation, joined in. Around and
around the chair they went, until Sam, uncertain whether
two against one was really a game, huddled for protection behind Tessa's legs.

Tessa ran forward and threw her arms around Cinnamon. "She's well," she said. "Isn't she well, Colin?"

"Better," said Colin cautiously. Then, with unusual excitement, "Hey, Tessa, stand aside a minute and let's see."

Tessa alarmed, moved away from the calf.

"What's wrong with her, Colin?" asked Jan as Colin
with his head on one side studied Cinnamon.

"What's wrong? What's right, you mean." His gruff
voice rose to its old boyish height with excitement. "I
never looked at her before."

"Oh, Colin," protested Tessa, who knew just how many
hours Colin had spent with Cinnamon.

"No, I never, not proper. Tessa, she's a real little
beaut."

"I know that," said Tessa loyally.

"No, I mean—aw, heck," Colin complained as he struggled to fit words to his thoughts. "She's a beaut, a cracker-
jack. Bet someone's kicking himself for losing this one's
mother."

"You mean," said Jan, "that she isn't a wild cow?"

"No such thing that I ever heard of."

"Oh, but Tessa, you can't keep another person's calf."

"But I love her," Tessa burst out. "You said, about
Aunt Helen's books . . ." But she knew that it was not the
same. The books were possessions that young Helen Duggan had loved once and outgrown; Cinnamon was part of
a man's livelihood. "Well, we don't know whose calf she
is, anyway," she argued.

She might not have been there, for all the notice they took of her.

"We oughter ask around," Colin told Jan. "I said so from the first, but she wouldn't listen."

"Why, it's a mystery," said Jan, her eyes dancing, and Tessa realized with despair that Jan was a person to whom mysteries were a challenge, not to be relinquished until they were solved. "Where do we start? Who might have lost her?" she asked Colin.

"Well, the way I work it out," said Colin, glowing at the chance that had made him Jan's equal and adviser, "is that she musta come from somewhere near—my grand-dad's, Ted Howarth's, or Riverlea—that's all there is back on to the bush—at least within a coupla miles."

"A couple of miles," Jan repeated thoughtfully. "Then, if you and Tessa take your bikes and I borrow Ruth's, we should be able to get around them all before lunch. Come on, Colin."

Nobody told Tessa to come on, and she followed silently as they walked along and made their plans. Colin would go to his grandfather's on one side of the farm while the two girls went in the opposite direction to Riverlea. Then whoever finished first would tackle the unpleasant Mr. Howarth.

EIGHT

Who Owns Cinnamon?

Mr. Sanderson was sitting on the veranda in the sunshine with a chessboard and a book in front of him on a little cane-legged table. It was not at all the way Tessa had been brought up to think that a farmer should behave at eleven o'clock on Monday morning. From the far side of the beautiful garden came the sound of a tractor as Young Pat went about the work of the farm.

He did not look up as the two girls leaned their bicycles against the veranda rail and climbed the broad steps. Perhaps the music that poured through the open windows behind him muffled their footsteps.

Jan coughed. "Excuse me, Mr. Sanderson," she said, while Tessa behind her nervously shuffled her feet and wished that there were some way of getting back to the time when they could decide not to come. Mr. Sanderson at home was a stranger.

He looked up, startled a moment, and then smiled. "I suppose it's too much to hope," he said, "that either of you young ladies is any good at chess problems."

Jan looked over his shoulder at the page of symbols which looked to Tessa like an eccentric knitting pattern. "I'm hopeless at problems," Jan said. "It's my mother you need."

"Am I to gather from that that you do play chess? That's a miracle in itself in this wilderness. Do lend your fresh young mind to this. You can't do worse than I have."

Encouraged, Jan bent over the chessboard and tentatively moved a piece. "No, that won't do," she said and replaced it.

In a moment they were absorbed in moving pieces, changing their minds, discussing the problem. Tessa fidgeted, impatient to get on to the reason of their visit. There was something foreign and alarming in the confidence with which Jan advised and even argued with the strange adult. In minutes their shared concern for the chess problem had them as much at ease as if they had known each other all their lives and Tessa, who was meant to be the friend of both, was an outsider, not even called on to introduce them.

"We didn't come here to play chess," she at last found the courage to remind Jan. "We came her to ask about a lost cow."

Mr. Sanderson turned at once from the chessboard. "Ah, yes," he said, the laughter lines beside his eyes deepening, "the imaginary cow. So it's become a real one, has it?"

"You knew," said Tessa angrily. It had been polite of him to pretend stupidity when the cow was a secret, but there was no need to make a game of it now. He was treating her like a child.

"You mustn't tease her," said Jan, taking her part, but as if she were Mr. Sanderson's grown-up friend protecting a child. She explained about the lost cow and Cinnamon and the way Tessa and Colin had saved Cinnamon's life.

Mr. Sanderson was interested. He asked one question after another but he did not say whether he had lost a cow.

"But have you lost one?" Tessa demanded, beside herself with suspense.

"I'm a bad farmer, Tessa. You ask your father. Young Pat's the man to tell you where the cows are and if all of them have got four legs."

"Come on, Jan," Tessa ran to the top of the steps. She

could still hear Young Pat's tractor among the farm
buildings.

"Hold on, chess player," said Mr. Sanderson as Jan
moved away. "I'm not letting you go before I even know
your name."

"She's my cousin Jan, and she's staying with us all this
week." Tessa had no time to put it more politely. As she
spoke, the engine of the tractor stopped. Young Pat might
go anywhere on the farm and, without the noise of the
tractor to guide them, they might never find him.

Mr. Sanderson looked at his watch. "Eleven o'clock to
the second—morning teatime. You could set your watch
by Young Pat. Don't worry, Tessa—Pat isn't going to
softly and silently vanish away, carrying all the statistics
of the Riverlea herd with him. And even I get stony looks
if I dare approach him about farm business in the sanc-
tuary of his morning tea break. So why not join me in a
cup of coffee and face him refreshed when he returns?"

As they followed him into the kitchen, a washing machine that had been whirling merrily flopped to a stand-
still. "More work," said Mr. Sanderson, looking with distaste at the limp clothes behind the machine's glass door.

Jan opened the door and began to take the washing out.
Tessa was alarmed at such a liberty in a stranger's house,
but when Mr. Sanderson explained, by way of apology for
the chaotic state of the kitchen, that, except for Mrs.
Howarth, who "flicked a duster over the furniture" two
mornings a week, he did all his own housework and cooking, she was so sorry for him that she found the clothespins
among a clutter of carpenter's tools on top of the refrigerator and ran to hold the door open for Jan as she carried
the clothes basket outside. She was shocked at the idea of
a man washing his own sheets and cooking his own dinner.
Her father was not expected to make as much as a cup

of tea for himself. If, as rarely happened, there was nobody to make it for him, he sat down and waited until
one of his womenfolk returned.

They hung up the clothes in silence. Jan was listening
intently to the music that still reached them through the
open window of the kitchen. At least Tessa supposed that
she was listening. People did listen to music, in books
anyway, although at home it was just something that came
out of the little transistor radio in the kitchen all day without anybody really noticing the noise, only the silence if it
was turned off. The music now was the sort Dad called
highbrow and always switched off.

Tessa listened too, and found she was enjoying the
sounds. "I think I'm turning into a highbrow," she said
as the music finished, dismayed by her own enjoyment.

"And would that be such a dreadful fate?" asked Mr.
Sanderson from the kitchen door. Tessa had not heard
him come out. She turned, blushing, and saw the smile on
his face. She thought he was laughing at her. Deliberately
she took down a shirt that Jan had pegged up by its
shoulders and hung it again by its tail so that the breeze
could catch it and it would not be pulled out of shape by
the clothespins. That at least she understood better than
Jan. Mr. Sanderson laughed as if he knew just why she
had done it.

"And what shall we give our newly converted highbrow
with her coffee?" he asked as they carried their mugs of
coffee through the room where a big record player stood.

Jan squatted down to examine the records that stood on
a rack against the wall. "What about this?" she asked,
holding out one of them.

"Do you think so, Jan, for a beginner?" asked Mr.
Sanderson.

"Well, it's one of the first things my mother played to

me, and I was much younger than Tessa. I just thought
. . ." Jan turned the record over as she spoke. Something
was written on the back. She read it slowly, then looked
at Mr. Sanderson. "I don't think we've been properly
introduced," she stammered in a manner very different
from that of the confident Jan that Tessa knew. "I'm—
well, I'm Janet Freeman. Well, I mean, Helen's writing
hasn't changed much in all these years."

A silence followed. Tessa, perplexed, moved closer to
Jan until she could read over her shoulder the words that
had produced such a strange effect. *Dear Dennis, with
all my love, Helen.* The ink had cracked on the shiny
surface. There was a date, *Christmas 195-,* but the last
figure had been rubbed off.

Mr. Sanderson took the record from Jan without saying
anything and put it on the player. Gay music followed
them onto the veranda. He put his mug of coffee on the
table and pulled out two canvas folding chairs. "She went
to England," he said.

"We came back again," said Jan, unnecessarily, Tessa
thought.

"She married an Englishman. I thought she'd settled
over there."

"He died two years later."

"I'm sorry."

"I never knew him. I was only a baby."

"And Helen—your mother—she hasn't married again?"

"No."

Nobody spoke again. They sat drinking their coffee and
listening to the music. Tessa, who had never had coffee
before, found it unpleasantly bitter and only the fear of
hurting Mr. Sanderson's feelings enabled her to gulp it
down. She listened to the music and although it was
probably as "highbrow" as the first record, she enjoyed it.

She was sorry when it finished and there was nothing to hear but the distant sound of Young Pat's tractor.

"Well," said Mr. Sanderson, getting up, "shall we consult the oracle before he drives off to the far end of the farm?"

"We'll wash the mugs for you," Tessa dutifully offered, although she longed to be off to see Young Pat.

"Ah, me, I'll never come up to your standards, Tessa. Around here we let the morning coffee cups keep the breakfast dishes company. They'll be done with the tea things at the latest—after lunch if I'm feeling like a good housewife. There, now, Tessa, I've shocked you, and you're supposed to be the farm-boy daughter. Just as well you didn't bring the domesticated one."

He chattered on to Tessa as they walked across the garden. When Jan paused to admire the spring flowers, he answered her briefly and then returned to Tessa. His friendship with Jan seemed to have ended as suddenly as it began.

They caught up with Young Pat as he was moving off along the drive. At a call from Mr. Sanderson he left his tractor and hurried back to join them.

"Pat," said Mr. Sanderson, "help me. I've completely lost the respect of young Tessa here and I'm likely to lose my self-respect unless I can win back her confidence. Please reassure her—and me—that our cows are safely counted and secure and not roaming about the bush dropping cinnamon-colored calves and then vanishing away."

"Eh?" Pat said. Tessa thought for a moment he was alarmed, then he went on, smiling amiably, "Is this some sort of joke, Mr. Sanderson? I'm sorry, but I don't quite get it."

Mr. Sanderson explained about Cinnamon and the search for her real owner. "And it's just occurred to me,

Pat," he said, "that a few weeks ago I did draw your attention to a gap in the fence of a paddock up by the bush, the very one, as it happens, in which we keep the expectant mums, or whatever technical terms we farmers are supposed to call them by. I suppose you did mend that gap?"

"Oh, at once, Mr. Sanderson. Worked till after dark that very night and moved the cows just to be on the safe side. Ted Howarth, who helped me, will bear me out. Lucky you noticed that, Mr. Sanderson, or we really might have cows vanishing into the bush and dropping calves like you said."

"And none of them escaped before you and Ted worked your overtime?"

"Cows missing and me not tell you, Mr. Sanderson?" Young Pat sounded hurt.

"They're valuable cows, the Riverlea herd, Pat. Irreplaceable, my brother used to say."

"I'd guard them with my life, Mr. Sanderson."

"I think well-kept fences should be sufficient and rather more practical."

"Too right, Mr. Sanderson." Young Pat grinned his appreciation of his employer's wit.

"That's all then, Pat. Thank you for your help." As Young Pat returned to his tractor Mr. Sanderson turned to Tessa and said, "Well, there you are, all present. So it isn't a Riverlea calf you've got." He looked back, frowning, at Young Pat. "I wonder if Colin has found anything. Let me know how things turn out, won't you? Jan, you can bring me news when you come over for that game of chess."

Jan, who had already begun to walk toward the house, pulled up short at the sound of her own name. "Do you still want me to?" she asked. "I thought that now you knew . . ."

Mr. Sanderson laughed. "That I wouldn't play chess with you because your mother and I were engaged in the dim, distant past? You've been watching too many old romantic movies on television, my girl. This is life, not Hollywood in the forties. Your mother and I fell in love and out again the best part of twenty years ago, and that has nothing whatever to do with the game of chess. Except that if Helen taught you, you should be a solid opponent. That girl played a damn good game—for a woman."

"Oh, so women can't play chess?" Jan said, laughing.

"I've heard that before, and paid for it, as your mother will tell you. Just bike over any day. Give me a ring to make sure I'm not out on the farm." He looked at Tessa, his eyes crinkling with laughter. "Despite what some people think, I do work from time to time when it's unavoidable."

"I don't know what to make of him," said Tessa as they pushed their bikes through the thick gravel of the Riverlea drive.

"Don't you?" said Jan. "He seems nice enough to me."

"But, Jan, why does he come to live on a farm if he doesn't want to work as a farmer?"

"Why should he, if he can afford to pay other men to do the work for him?"

Tessa gave up. Perhaps where Jan came from, work was not the most important thing. She had often heard her father and his friends complain about lazy townees with their forty-hour week who never had to stay up half the night delivering a calf and then be in the milking shed

before seven with a twelve-hour day at least before them.
The farmers complained of the hard work as if they
would take any opportunity to escape, and yet they despised anyone who worked less hard than they. They
despised Mr. Sanderson. "At least he noticed the broken
fence," she said aloud to comfort herself. "But Mr. Graham
Sanderson knew so much about cows," she added sadly.

"I do think Helen might have warned me," said Jan as
if, intent on her own thoughts, she had not taken in a
word that Tessa said.

Colin was leaning on his bicycle at the Howarths' front
gate. On the other side of the fence, with their arms
folded along its top, stood Mr. Howarth, Billy, and Warren. At their feet a grubby little girl with a fistful of mud
that she had been about to eat paused to poke out her
tongue at Colin, while a small boy hauled himself with
black and sticky hands up the leg of his jeans. Colin
looked most unhappy. As the two girls coasted down the
hill from Riverlea, the expression on his face as he
watched them was a silent cry for help.

"Yeah, that's right," Mr. Howarth was saying as they
came close enough to hear. "A sort of yellowish color,
real light for a Jersey, sorta shading to gray on her nose
and legs."

Tessa stopped dead and stared at him. She had not told
Colin about the gray shading. She had not even thought
of it herself. It was the rich honey-gold of the cow's back
that had struck her, but now the gray muzzle and legs
were as clear to her as if she sat again in the fork of the
tree and watched the cow pushing through the undergrowth below.

"Oh," said Jan brightly, "is there a clue at last then?
Do you know something about her, Mr. Howarth?"

"Should do after the hours me and the boys spent trailing through the bush lookin' for her."

"Sure thing," said Warren. But Billy, who was not very bright, just stared at his father, breathing hard through a wide-open mouth.

Jan's quick eye glanced from Mr. Howarth to Warren to Billy and then remained watching the boy until he self-consciously shuffled his feet and giggled. "Do you remember helping search for your father's cow?" she asked him.

Billy looked with frightened eyes at his father.

"Y'know, Bill," said Warren helpfully, "when Dad shot that old goat."

Billy's face brightened as his slow mind tracked down the memory. "Yeah. Smashin'. Bang—down she fell like in the pictures. Bang, bang, she's dead."

The smallest Howarth, squatting at Colin's feet and picking caked mud from his boots, looked up with interest. "Bang, you're dead," he said, aiming a muddy finger at Jan.

"And bang, you're dead, too." Jan with a look of distaste returned his fire.

"She can't do that," the small Howarth wailed through a nose badly in need of wiping. "I deaded her first. Lie down, you rotten cheat!"

Above a shriek of "Lie down!" from the three younger Howarths, Jan shouted at their father, "I suppose you know that goat had a young kid that wasn't weaned?"

"Yeah, I'm not blind. So what? Two pests less to destroy the native trees."

Colin stepped forward, sending a couple of small Howarths sprawling in the mud. His thrust-out jaw almost touched Mr. Howarth's face, but it was some time before he could find words to fit his anger. Ted Howarth waited as if unconcerned by the boy's face inches from his own

and scarlet with anger. "Goats is a menace," Colin said at
last, "but so's a man that shoots off his gun at every living
thing. Nobody as can help it shoots a mother and leaves
its baby to starve. And what about Sanderson's sheepdog?
Was that doin' harm to the native trees?"

That was an old story, going back to the time of Mr.
Graham Sanderson, which Tessa had forgotten until now.
There had been talk of poor light and the dangers of stray
dogs, but nobody had believed it. Ted Howarth had no
sheep to make him fear killer dogs, just a light finger on
the trigger when he saw any moving creature. His own
stock he fed because they were his livelihood; anything
else that moved was fair game. And this was the man who
claimed to own weak little Cinnamon, who still needed
gentleness and care.

"She can't be yours," Tessa burst out. "She was beautiful—she was a well-bred cow."

"Yeah," said Mr. Howarth, "that's the sort of attitude
I'd expect from you lot. 'It can't be yours, Ted Howarth,
it's a decent beast. Townee Sanderson can keep good
stock but not you, Ted Howarth, what's got half a dozen
kids that might starve for all anyone cares. Any old
wreck's good enough for you.' "

Tessa had not meant to say all that. She might not like
the Howarths, but she certainly didn't want them to
starve.

"Does anyone except Warren and you know you lost a
cow?" asked Jan.

"Like I said, they'd only laugh at a man for trying to
improve his herd. I mighta told me mate, Pat Duggan.
I might even 'a showed him the cow before it got lost. I
don't rightly remember."

"You see," Jan went on, "Tessa and Colin have worked

hard night and day to save the calf's life. We want to be sure she goes back to the right owner."

"Oh, sure, half the farmers in the district have lost cows roaming around the bush, well-bred animals like what Colin says, like what I saved up for and then lost. Like I described right, didn't I? I suppose a man's word of honor isn't good enough for you, young Miss Whoever you are."

Jan with dignity told him her name. She looked smaller and frailer than ever as she faced the big, scowling man. Colin, with clenched fists bulging in his pockets, stood protectively behind her. "You haven't lost a cow, Ted Howarth," she said.

"And how do you work that out, Miss Janet Freeman?"

"Billy didn't know anything about it."

"Billy aren't all there. Are you, Bill?"

"Naw," said Billy happily.

"And Warren isn't telling the truth."

"Hey, hold on, you," protested Warren.

"Very well, Warren, you just tell me when the cow broke her horn."

Warren looked from his father to Jan and then back to his father. "When did she, Dad?" he asked.

"Oh, yeah," said Mr. Howarth confidently, "that broken horn. I'd sorta forgotten that. Proves my story, don't it? This cow of mine, she had a broken horn right enough. Broke it one day fighting with another cow. You must remember that, Warren."

"Oh, I remember now," said Warren obediently.

"Then I'm afraid there must be two lost cows in the bush after all," said Jan sweetly. "Yours had two perfectly good horns, didn't she, Tessa?"

"She had no horns at all," said Tessa, who had been

worrying over that fact while they discussed the imaginary horn.

"You little . . ." It would have been no trouble at all for Mr. Howarth to pick up Jan by the scruff of her neck and shake her like a puppy and for a moment he seemed to intend just that. Then he laughed huskily. "Worth trying, eh?" he said. "After the praise young Colin here was giving that calf. A man's got to look after hisself in this world."

Jan turned away from him with a look of distaste and picked up her bicycle. Tessa and Colin followed. As they cycled away, Tessa heard Billy's adenoidal voice say, "Aren't they gonner give us the wee calf, Dad?" A slap of hand against ear followed and then Billy's voice was raised in a loud wail. She would have given Cinnamon to anyone rather than the Howarths.

She pedaled hard to catch up with Colin. "Uncle Alec —he's sure she's not his?" she asked.

"Positive."

She had known what the answer would be, but she was so delighted to hear it spoken, and with such certainty, that she lifted her hands from the handlebars and let out a whoop of joy as she swerved dangerously around a bend in the road.

Jan creaked up to them, panting as she fought to get speed out of Ruth's old bike. Against the wind of their movement, Tessa heard her shout something about a mystery. Let Jan have her mystery, she thought. She was content that she still had Cinnamon.

NINE

Ruth Spies

Except when she borrowed Ruth's bicycle and went off to Riverlea to play chess with Mr. Sanderson, Jan went everywhere with Tessa. She became quite a useful person to have about the farm. Dad said so and his praise was not easily given.

Often when they were not needed to help with the farm work, the two girls sat for hours together on the veranda of Grandpa Pat's house, reading, or, their books forgotten, laughing together at the games of Cinnamon, Nutmeg, and Sam. Colin, when he had time, was always welcome there with his knowledge of the rearing of young animals. But Ruth was never asked. Tessa felt that she was too much in league with Mum to be trusted to keep the secret of Cinnamon and Nutmeg and although Jan sometimes argued that it was unfair that three should have a secret and one be left out, she had to admit that the animals were Tessa's and it was she who had the right to decide who should be told about them and who not.

The last full day of Jan's week at the farm came more quickly than anyone could have imagined and still they were no nearer to finding Cinnamon's owner, to the disappointment of Jan, who loved to solve mysteries, and the relief of Tessa, who loved Cinnamon. On their last afternoon together the three friends sat on Grandpa Pat's veranda. Near them lay Cinnamon and Nutmeg, back to back and half asleep in the sunshine, with Sam squatting beside them, his nose between his paws.

"And we still don't know how Mr. Howarth knew the color of Cinnamon's mother," said Tessa, "unless he was telling the truth."

"He wasn't," said Jan decidedly. "But I'm sure there's something suspicious about your Mr. Howarth. He and Young Pat. Aren't those two as thick as thieves and doesn't Howarth do a bit of work for Dennis Sanderson? If it was Dennis's cow and if Young Pat was lying . . ."

From the top step Colin interrupted her with a shout: "Ruth! Hiding in the scrub!"

"Grab her!" Tessa leaped down the steps and obeyed her own command.

"I'll tell," Ruth panted as they tussled together among the manuka bushes. "Where did you get that calf? I'm telling Dad." She gave Tessa a push that sent her sprawling on the ground and ran toward the house.

"Why didn't you stop her?" Tessa demanded of her two friends as she sat up and tenderly rubbed her bruised arms. "She'll tell everything now."

Jan laughed down at her from the veranda. "Tessa, you do look a sight. Now calm down and think. She's seen and she'll tell sooner or later unless you're planning to keep her a prisoner in Grandpa Pat's house for the rest of her life. If I were you, I'd get along to Uncle Joe and confess before she gets a chance to tell him. It's your only hope of getting off lightly now."

She laughed again and Colin joined in with his gruff, foolish "haw-haw." They had always wanted to tell Dad. As she turned her back on them and trudged across the farm, Tessa could not even remember why it had been so important that he should not be told. In the last few days she had been so absorbed in her friends, animal and human, that her quarrel with Dad had faded into the past. The whole secret seemed pointless now, and yet she well knew that there would be trouble when it was told, just because it had been a secret for so long.

Ruth was already in the cowyard talking to Dad when Tessa came up sheepishly behind him.

"Here she is now," said Ruth. "You just ask her if she hasn't got a calf in Grandpa Pat's house. And a goat. Honest, Dad, she's got a regular zoo."

Dad turned and looked at Tessa. The expression on his face was not reassuring. "Where'd you get a calf?" he asked.

"In the bush," Tessa mumbled.

"When was this? Some time this morning? Why wasn't I told?"

Tessa looked at the concrete yard, intently studying a line of grass that grew along a crack. "The week before last."

By the time that Jan and Colin strolled up, Dad had learned enough to be in a shouting rage. He turned on the newcomers. "And you two, surely you're old enough to have a bit of sense," he told them.

"It wasn't Tessa's fault," said Jan. "Every time she tried to tell you, you were so angry already that she was scared to make things worse. She just wanted to stay friends with you, Uncle Joe."

"A nice way she's gone about it, I must say. No, Tessa, this is just part and parcel with your behavior lately. Plain disobedience, that's all."

"You're refusing to see her point of view," said Jan.

"Tessa and Colin know what I'm talking about. They deliberately risked the life of a young animal, keeping it in that drafty old ruin with only a couple of kids to look after it. I thought you at least had more concern for animals, Colin, than to leave even some miserable little stray . . ."

"Cinnamon aren't no miserable stray," said Colin, more indignant at the insult to Cinnamon than the attack on himself. "You just come and see, Uncle Joe."

Dad had to do some more shouting before he was calm enough to go with them to Grandpa Pat's house. Ruth followed, smug but more isolated than ever.

Dad's rage had shouted itself out. The last sparks died as he saw Cinnamon. Nearly a week of Nutmeg's company had improved her far beyond the calf that Colin had first noticed as well bred. Her coat had the beginning of a shine to it over sides that were becoming rounded, her eyes were bright and gentle and her nose shone with healthy moisture. Dad looked at her greedily. "I could use an animal like that," he said. Then, with a visible battle, his honesty took over. "Somebody's certainly sore at losing this one. I wonder who. Y'know, Colin, I reckon she wouldn't be no disgrace to Riverlea."

Jan told him about their visit to Mr. Sanderson.

"Well, I wouldn't trust Dennis Sanderson to know if he'd lost every animal on the place, but Young Pat knows his job. I'll take his word any day." He paused and Tessa wondered if he was thinking of the result of taking Young Pat's word about the Riverlea bull. "Young Pat's a good lad," he said at last, as if somebody had suggested otherwise.

"Mr. Howarth said it was his cow," said Tessa.

Dad laughed at Ted Howarth's attempt to claim Cinnamon. "Just like his nerve," he said. "Well, you can bet your bottom dollar this calf wasn't bred from none of his stock. So if it isn't Riverlea and it isn't Alec's—you asked Granddad, Colin?—and, more's the pity, it isn't mine. We can only put an ad in the paper and hope the owner hasn't given up after all this time." He gave Tessa a disapproving look, but she was too miserable to notice it. She had hoped her father's admiration for the calf would prove stronger than his honesty, for, however hard she tried, she could not feel that the unknown farmer who had let his cow stray into the bush had more right to Cinnamon than the person who had saved her life.

Colin, quietly efficient in farming matters, had brought a halter from the barn. He slipped it over Cinnamon's head and led her down the steps. Nutmeg skipped after them.

"And this animal," said Dad, "can go back to the bush where it belongs."

It was the moment that Tessa had been fearing. She had thought out Nutmeg's defense long ago. "Goats are useful," she said. "They eat rank grass that a cow wouldn't and they give milk. I could milk her myself," she added quickly in case Dad thought that Nutmeg would mean extra work for himself.

"On a dairy farm we don't need to live on goat's milk. She goes back to the bush."

"Uncle Joe," protested Jan, "I didn't think you could be so mean. Why shouldn't Tessa have just one pet?"

"Seems like she's made one of my cattle dog already," said Dad as he watched Sam dance around Tessa's feet. "It's been nothin' but pet dog, pet calf, pet kid, all these holidays. That's her year's ration."

"But what harm could one little goat do you? She could live in that little paddock beside the house and you'd never know she was there," Jan argued.

Tessa looked hopefully at her father. The narrow paddock beside the house was too small for grazing stock. A few tree tomatoes and a lemon tree had given it the grand name of orchard, but in terms of farming it was just waste ground. "Please, Dad," she said. "Cinnamon will be miserable without Nutmeg."

"That's right, Uncle Joe," Colin said. "Like when we had to fetch old Nutty from the bush because the little calf was pining without her."

"She'll have the other calves," said Dad.

"And Tessa will have nothing," said Jan.

"Tessa don't deserve nothin'. She knows that. I dunno how my sister brought you up with all her educated notions, but around here we don't give rewards for plain, stubborn disobedience."

"Helen never robbed me of something I loved just because she was in a bad mood. If that's an educated notion, then I'm glad my mother went to the university instead of staying here to become just another ignorant country bumpkin."

"I may be a country bumpkin," snarled Dad, "but I'm not in a bad mood, and if I am, I've every right to be."

"That isn't logical, Uncle Joe."

"Since when do I have to be accountable to every spoiled brat that comes to stay?"

"Just try to be reasonable, Uncle Joe. You're not being reasonable, you're just trying to hurt Tessa. And do you know why? It isn't because she disobeyed you, it's because you know that she and Colin did as good a job of calf rearing as you could yourself and you don't want to admit it. You're jealous of them, Uncle Joe. That's one of your reasons for being unfair. And the second is that you know it was your fault that Tessa was too frightened of you and your uncontrolled temper to tell you about the calf. You're ashamed of yourself and you won't admit it, so you take it out on Tessa instead."

Dad's face became white and drawn with anger as he listened. Tessa had never seen him look so angry. "Don't you speak to me like that," he said. His voice was quiet at first but it rose steadily until he was shouting. "You get inside. Go on. Go and stay in your room until I send for you. While you're in my house I'm responsible for you and I will not have that sort of insolence from you or any other child. Trying to tell me what I think and don't think! If that's the way Helen lets you speak to her, then I'm sorry for her, but while you're under my roof I'll take no more lip from you than I would from Ruth or Tessa. What you need, my girl, is a father to thrash a few of your cocky ways out of you, and if I hear another word I'll take my belt and do the job myself."

Jan in her turn grew very white. She opened her mouth to say something, then turned without a word toward the house.

Dad stood for a moment looking after her. Then he also turned aside, but not to follow Jan. "Come on, Colin," he said. "I reckon our best way's to let her follow her little friend into the orchard, then lead Cinnamon out and shut the gate. It wouldn't be doing them no kindness to leave them together when Cinnamon'll be off in a few days and put straight in with other calves as like as not. Poor little devil probably don't know she is a calf after the company she's kept." His anger had shouted itself out. He spoke like a man exhausted and defeated.

Tessa stayed in the orchard comforting a bleating Nutmeg until milking time. After milking she went into the sunroom to tidy her hair before tea, a habit to which Ruth's comments rather than any desire for neatness had driven her. Jan lay on her bed sobbing. Tessa stood in the middle of the floor and stared uncomfortably. All Jan's three years of seniority stood between them and she felt very young and very helpless. "Jan," she said timidly, "Dad's letting me keep Nutmeg." That, after all, had been the reason for the quarrel, and Jan should be pleased to know that she had won. But she gave no sign of having heard.

Tessa quietly left the room, her hair still unbrushed. In the kitchen her mother, the one person who could always be relied on in trouble, was making gravy. Without a word, when Tessa had told her of Jan's distress, she brushed flour from her hands and went through into the sunroom.

At the same time Dad and Ruth both came into the kitchen. Tessa busied herself with the half-made gravy and then dished out their sausages. Nobody asked where Mum and Jan were. They ate in silence, as if the unhappiness on the other side of the wall somehow seeped through and depressed them all.

They had finished and the girls were washing the dishes before Mum came out of the sunroom. "Well, Joe Duggan," she said, "I hope you're proud of yourself." Tessa had never seen her mother so close to anger. She took Jan's sausages from the oven, set them out on a tray with bread and butter and tea and took them through into the sunroom.

Dad put down his newspaper and walked to the sunroom door. Then he walked away again. "If that little minx thinks I'm going to apologize," he said, "then she's got another think coming." He picked up his newspaper and rustled through it savagely, as if fighting rather than reading it. The girls went on with the dishes.

At last Mum returned with the tray nearly as full as when she had taken it in. In silence she helped herself to her own tea. The room was so still that they could hear Nutmeg's heartbroken bleats from the orchard. Once Tessa thought she heard from far away in the calf paddock an equally sorrowful reply.

Dad threw down his paper and went to the back door. He put on his boots and went out, slamming the door behind him. "What's got into the man now?" asked Mum. "No cows due to calve, are there, Tessa?"

Tessa shook her head. She was listening still to the bleating in the orchard. Suddenly it stopped.

A few minutes later Dad returned. "I hope you're satisfied," he told Tessa. "Either that calf thinks she's a goat or I don't know what. I only hope her real owner, whoever he is, can persuade her otherwise." He made for his chair, then turned aside like a tacking yacht and headed for the sunroom door instead. It was a long time before he returned with a red-eyed and subdued but apparently friendly Jan.

Dad did not stop in the kitchen. Without a word to anyone, he went through into the hall and shut the door behind him. They heard the telephone tinkle as he dialed a number.

Jan presumably knew what was going on, but nobody dared intrude on her white-faced, tear-stained silence by asking. They waited until Dad returned.

"Well, that's settled, Jan," he said cheerfully. "Helen says of course you can stay until the end of the holidays and she'll drive over on next Sunday to collect you and Ruth. Okay?"

Jan's smile was pale and forced but it was a smile and aimed at Dad. "Thank you so much, Uncle Joe," she said.

"That's all right," said Dad uncomfortably. "If I'd 'a known you was upset already about goin' home. . . . Oh, never mind." He hurled himself into his chair and took shelter behind his outspread newspaper.

TEN

"Found—Jersey Calf"

The advertisements which appeared in the two New Plymouth papers on Monday gave both the telephone number and the address at which the lost calf could be claimed. Either the sound of a car on the road or the telephone bell became sounds of dread to Tessa. School had started for her, though not for the high school children, and she returned home each afternoon in fear that Cinnamon would be already gone.

As much of her free time as possible she spent in the orchard, where she both enjoyed Cinnamon's company and kept an eye on the house. Jan often joined her there, and so did Colin when his farm work allowed. Ruth, unsure of her welcome, brought Nutmeg such delicacies from the kitchen as apple peel and carrot scrapings.

As the days passed, Tessa began to hope again. By Saturday it seemed reasonable to suppose that Cinnamon's owner had not seen the advertisement. Then, as they were sitting down to dinner, the front door bell rang. Only strangers rang front door bells in Manurima. Anybody they knew would come to the back door and call "Coo-ee!"

Tessa was out of the kitchen before anyone else had moved, determined to hear the worst and get it over. It was a hot day and the front door stood open, so that as soon as she was in the hall she could see Mr. Sanderson standing on the porch and beside him, although Tessa scarcely noticed her at first, Jenny Wren.

"Oh no," she exclaimed, her mind still on Cinnamon, "Young Pat hasn't changed his mind!"

Mum came bustling down the hall. "Where are your manners, Tessa, leaving people on the doorstep? Do come in, Mr. Sanderson, Miss Renfrew."

"Thank you," said Mr. Sanderson, "but we were just passing and dropped in for a moment. I wanted Tessa to show Miss Renfrew her little calf. I feel she should see what her pupils get up to in the holidays."

See what she got up to in the holidays! Tessa was horrified. Wasn't it bad enough having Jenny Wren all term without having her poke her nose into holiday affairs?

None of that could be said aloud, however, and in sulky silence she led them through a little gate under an arch of macrocarpa hedge and into the orchard.

"But that isn't a calf, it's a kid," said Jenny Wren as Nutmeg bounced toward them.

Tessa just looked at her. Her spelling and arithmetic might go astray at times, but she knew that on the subject of cows there was a lot she could teach Jenny Wren.

"There she is, over there by that tree-tomato tree." Mr. Sanderson walked quietly toward Cinnamon, calling to her. "Come on then, old girl, come and be admired. Why, Tessa, she's a little beauty!"

And how would you know? Tessa mentally asked him.

As if she had spoken her thought aloud, he laughed and said, "You don't have a brother as wrapped up in cows as mine was without learning something about the points to look for. Doesn't your father think she comes from good stock?"

"He thinks she's good enough to be yours," said Tessa unwillingly.

"I wish she were. Well now, Tessa, I want you to tell

Miss Renfrew all you and Jan told me, about how you and
Colin taught the calf to drink and about those all-night
vigils in the old house."

Tessa, aware that Jenny Wren was listening without
interest and with more than one glance at her watch, muttered her way uncomfortably through the story.

"Isn't it an achievement, Jennifer?" said Mr. Sanderson
enthusiastically. "Now how would your clever, docile town
kids cope with a situation like that?"

"Town children would hardly get themselves into the
situation," said Jenny Wren coldly.

"Exactly. Different children, different experiences, and
you can't hope to succeed unless you accept them as they
are. Tessa's out helping to earn the family's living each
morning when your city kids are still asleep with Mother
to call them and find their clothes and cook their breakfast. She's a responsible, capable young woman, not a child
with nothing to worry about except her schoolwork."

"But I still can't spell," said Tessa, who felt that she
had been praised enough for things that were a normal
part of life.

Mr. Sanderson ignored her spelling. "You must see,
Jennifer," he said. "It's a challenge."

"It's very interesting," said Jenny Wren in an exceed-
ingly uninterested tone. "Shall we go now, Dennis?"

But while Mr. Sanderson was lecturing Jenny Wren, the
little paddock had become quite crowded. Not only had
the family finished their dinner and come out, but Uncle
Harold Ritchie, Trevor, and the Hope brothers had arrived, having read, as they explained, the advertisement
and driven over to see the stray calf. Mr. Sanderson was
soon the center of a little group as he retold Tessa's story
to a much more appreciative audience than Jenny Wren.

Cinnamon took their admiration calmly enough, but

Tessa was embarrassed. She slid out of the crowd to join Jan and Ruth, who were by the road fence feeding black-berry shoots to Nutmeg.

"I like your Miss Renfrew," said Ruth. "She's pretty and she dresses well."

"Huh," said Tessa.

"Insipid," pronounced Jan, "but pretty enough in a washed-out sort of way. She certainly seems to have made an impression on poor Dennis."

"He doesn't like the way she teaches me," said Tessa.

"Sheep farmers' wives don't have to teach," said Ruth in her most crushing voice.

Tessa looked at Mr. Sanderson and Jenny Wren, but could see no cause for alarm on Mr. Sanderson's behalf. He was talking enthusiastically to the farmers while she laughed loudly at some joke with Bernie Hope. Teen-agers like Ruth and Jan, she decided, saw romance everywhere.

She was so lost in her thoughts that she jumped when from behind her the friendly voice of Young Pat said, "That's as fine a job of calf rearing as I've seen, Tessa. Congratulations."

Tessa turned to face the frank, white-toothed smile of her cousin. In an open-necked shirt, with a jacket swung across his shoulder, he looked very young and fresh and dependable, especially as he brought with him, as al-ways, the lowering contrast of Ted Howarth. "If ever I saw the result of real love and care, that's it," he went on. "I'll take you on as a farmhand any day, Tessa, Riverlea herd and all."

"Fine job, sure enough," growled Mr. Howarth, with-out taking his greedy eyes from Cinnamon.

"Did you find your broken-horned cow, Mr. Howarth?" Jan asked sweetly.

Ted Howarth scowled at her.

"You lost a cow, Ted?" Young Pat's voice was rich with silent laughter. "Hard luck, man. Told the kids when they came inquiring about Cinnamon and her ma, I suppose?"

"Strayed into a back paddock," muttered Mr. Howarth. "Found her next day."

"How annoying for you," said Jan, "when you and the boys had searched so long in the bush for her."

Young Pat laughed so loudly that the other men came over to share the joke. He shared it gleefully while Mr. Howarth scowled at everyone. Young Pat seemed really to enjoy his comrade's discomfort. It was an odd friendship, Tessa thought.

Mum had disappeared some time ago and Ruth had followed. Now she returned to say that there was a cup of tea in the kitchen for anyone who wanted it. Except for Mr. Howarth, who said that he had a farm to look after and didn't spend his afternoons gossiping over cups of tea like an old woman, they all trooped into the kitchen.

The conversation over tea was still about Cinnamon and the mystery of her ownership. There was not a man who did not agree that she was a well-bred animal.

"Looks like you're a lucky girl, Tessa," said Uncle Harold. "Shame you can't produce a pedigree for her, but, even so, she's a great addition to your father's stock. Make up a bit for the Riverlea bull, eh, Joe?"

Dad could not be depressed even by the mention of the Riverlea bull. He was a proud man. Tessa's disobedience was forgotten. She had brought him a calf that everyone admired, she had cared for it like a farmer whom the other farmers respected. Even Nutmeg, whose friendship with the calf tickled the men's sense of the absurd, had a share

in the glory. He beamed when they praised Ruth's baking.
"They're two good girls," Tessa heard him tell Mr. Sanderson. "Though I say it meself, there's not many a man
could boast of a better pair of daughters."

From the bedroom Daniel's voice was raised in a loud
wail. Who cares about you, young farmer? Tessa told him
silently and then was ashamed of the thought. He was,
after all, only a little helpless baby. She was glad when
Mum picked him up and brought him out into the kitchen
to be admired. He really did look rather sweet now that
he was becoming more like a human being. Tessa held out
her arms. Mum looked surprised as she handed Daniel
over, for Tessa had always refused to hold him. But Tessa
was happy enough to forget their rivalry and accept Daniel
as a delightfully plump and cuddly baby brother.

"Tessa."

She vaguely realized that it was the second time Jan had
spoken to her and she had been too absorbed in her
brother to listen.

"Tessa, Dennis wants to know if you and I would like
to go back to Riverlea with him and Jen—Miss Renfrew
to listen to some music."

She was too shy to refuse, and her shyness grew painfully
as they left the familiar kitchen and farmers' talk and
drove to Riverlea. Jenny Wren seemed unaware of her
existence, and Jan, in the company of her friend, "Dennis," seemed as grown up as the girl who had frightened
her on the first day of her visit.

She took the glass of orange juice that Mr. Sanderson
offered her and sat uncomfortably on the edge of a low
chair. Jenny Wren with a glass of sherry in her hand
walked about the room admiring everything, from the
view through a window to the fabric that covered a chair,

while Jan, as if quite at home, knelt down beside the
record rack and argued with Mr. Sanderson about what
music they should have.

"Behave yourself, child," said Mr. Sanderson. "You've
had your turn almost every day of the last week. Let somebody else have a chance to decide. What would you like to
hear, Jennifer?"

Jenny Wren smiled down at him. "I'm sure I'll enjoy
whatever pleases you, Dennis," she said.

Jan gave her a pitying look and handed a record to Mr.
Sanderson.

Suddenly Tessa jumped and nearly fell from her inse-
cure perch on the chair. Music was everywhere. When they
sat on the veranda it had all come from one direction, and
she had not thought of it as being very different from listening to the radio at home. But in the living room they
seemed to be right in the middle of the music.

Jenny Wren turned from the window to say something
about marvelous stereo equipment and then, since Mr.
Sanderson seemed unwilling to continue the conversation,
turned back to her contemplation of the Riverlea garden,
her fingers tapping restlessly on the windowpane.

Once she turned and caught Tessa's eye and a smile of
understanding passed between them such as Tessa could
never have imagined sharing with Jenny Wren. While Jan
and Mr. Sanderson sat motionless, absorbed in the music,
they were like conspirators, not disliking the sounds that
filled the room but unused to listening and both of
them, for different reasons, anxious to hide their boredom.
Another smile of rather guilty thankfulness passed between them when at last the music stopped.

Jan flopped down on her knees and began to search for
another record. "I can't find anything worthy to follow
that," she complained.

Mr. Sanderson got down beside her and took a record from the rack. Jan shook her head. They argued together while Jenny Wren glared at the backs of their heads.

"Dennis," she said.

There was no answer.

"Dennis, I'm looking forward to some more music, of course. You know how I love music. But don't you think it's unfair to this poor child to keep her sitting listening on a fine afternoon?"

Mr. Sanderson looked up at Tessa. "Of course," he said. "What am I thinking of? Wouldn't you rather be out playing in the garden, Tessa?"

That "playing" might have been spoken to a child of seven. Rather stiffly, Tessa said, "It must be nearly milking time. Can I go and see the Riverlea cows please, Mr. Sanderson? I've never seen them close up."

Mr. Sanderson laughed. "You and your cows! Off you go, then, and see if you can find anything there as beautiful as your Cinnamon."

She ran out and across the garden, with the music still dancing through her head and welcome now that it no longer demanded stillness.

The cows were in, and both Young Pat and Mr. Howarth were with them, but neither man seemed inclined for work. Mr. Howarth was sprawled on some bales of straw with a loud transistor radio close to his ear while Young Pat leaned against the rump of a cow that stood patiently in her stall waiting to be milked. Under the loud music the two men were talking earnestly, until the barking of Young Pat's sheepdog drew their attention to the visitor.

Young Pat strode across and switched off the radio. "Time we got some work done, Ted," he told Mr. Howarth. "That noise is enough to curdle the milk in the buckets. Right, Tessa?" He turned on his most charm-

ing smile. "Can't spoil your ear for the boss's classics with
that muck. Or have you run away from Mozart and
Beethoven and that lot?"

Tessa smiled shyly back at him. "Sort of," she said. "I
wanted to see the Riverlea herd close up."

"You what?" asked Mr. Howarth, sitting up straight.

"She wanted to see the Riverlea herd. Tessa's very interested in livestock."

"I suppose so," said Mr. Howarth and sprawled back
on his bales of straw.

Young Pat grinned at Tessa as if they shared a joke.
"Ted can't see livestock except as a walking bank bal-
lance," he said. "Can't see that anybody could just find
pleasure in looking at a good beast. Well, Tessa, there
they are, the famous Riverlea herd. Like them?"

Tessa had never been so close to the famous animals
before. Their coats shone like velvet, so soft that she
wanted to lay her cheek against them. Several turned to
look at her with mild brown eyes, so different from those
of their relation, the Riverlea bull. Whoever had taught
him to be treacherous and cowardly had not harmed the
tempers of the cows. "Oh, Pat, they're beautiful!" she said.
She wondered which was the famous Riverlea Princess. She
had seen her once, her neck swathed in championship
ribbons, being led around the show ring in the grand
parade at the end of the annual livestock show, a distant,
pale vision that had made her proud to be a neighbor of
Riverlea and to know Mr. Graham Sanderson. But she
could not pick her out among the beautiful cows. "Which
is Princess, please?" she asked.

"Eh?" Mr. Howarth sprang up from the bales and
glowered down at Tessa. "What are you up to, eh? Interfering kids!"

Tessa backed away, alarmed by his reaction to her innocent question.

"Princess?" said Young Pat in a soft voice. "She isn't in milk yet, Tessa. Quite a few of our cows haven't calved yet. I suppose some of your father's haven't? How about you, Ted, you got cows still to calf?"

He had to repeat the question before Mr. Howarth growled, "Tha's right."

"So you'll have to come some other day and see Princess. And maybe her calf too. I'd take you to see the calves we've got but I think I hear a car starting up. Must be the boss's blond girl friend leaving, so the party's breaking up and they'll be looking for you."

Tessa was hustled out of the milking shed, smiled on by Young Pat and glowered at by Mr. Howarth.

If Young Pat had heard a car it was not Jenny Wren's because Tessa as she left the farm buildings could see her wandering alone on the sloping lawn. She was on her way back to tell Young Pat the good news when it occurred to her that it might not be good news to him or news at all. He had dismissed her charmingly but he had dismissed her and because of a car that she had not heard and which certainly could not have been Jenny Wren's. From Ted Howarth she would not have expected charm, but to the unpleasantness that was natural to him there had been added a nervousness that was not. He had not liked her interest in Riverlea Princess.

Something was wrong. She could not imagine what it might be, but she knew there was a mystery about the Riverlea herd and at once, without knowing why or how, she connected it with the other mystery that had so occupied her thoughts, the mystery of Cinnamon.

She turned back, excited by a question that she dared

not ask Young Pat. Riverlea Princess! She was too proud
on Cinnamon's behalf to realize that, just as she had felt
safely the owner of Cinnamon, it would mean that a possible owner had been found.

Jenny Wren was still walking across the lawn and Tessa
panted up to her, so excited that she felt she must share
her discovery with the first person she met.

She poured out her story as she could never have imagined pouring out anything to Jenny Wren.

"You've at least got a lively imagination," said Jenny
Wren, "but you really must learn to control it. Too many
trashy books in which children solve mysteries and outwit
villains."

"But there *is* a mystery," she protested, "there's a cow
lost in the bush and most likely dead now that nobody
owns."

"Tessa, think. Which is more likely to be missing and
unclaimed, a valuble cow, or an ordinary one that nobody cares very much about? You're letting all the praise
you heard this afternoon go to your head, aren't you,
Tessa? Trying to make something special out of your
little calf."

Tessa could not find an answer to that. Perhaps, after all,
Jenny Wren was right and it was her imagination that
was wrong or the books she read or just the fact of being
Tessa Duggan. It was not unusual for her to feel when
faced with Jenny Wren that she had been born the wrong
person.

She hardly dared after that to tell Jan. It was not until
bedtime, the time for secrets, that she found courage
enough to give a timid account of her discovery. "Jenny
Wren says I read too much trash and have too much

imagination," she added generously, making the way easy for Jan to say the same.

"Jenny Wren wouldn't know an imagination if she tripped over one," said Jan in an assured, adult manner that alarmed Tessa. "It's suspicious, Tessa, everything about Pat Duggan and Ted Howarth is suspicious. *Could* your lost cow have been Riverlea Princess?"

Tessa nodded. She had spent most of the evening making mental comparisons between the cow she had seen briefly in the bright sunlight of the show ring and the one she had seen just as briefly in the gloom of the bush. They were both light-colored for Jerseys; they could be the same. "But Young Pat says she hasn't calved yet and Cinnamon was born weeks ago," she objected.

"Young Pat's too mealymouthed to be true. And if Dennis Sanderson doesn't wake up to it soon, he'll be ruined."

"Ruined?" Tessa echoed. Ruin was something that faced Dad when butter prices fell or a cow took sick, but she had never thought of it as facing a wealthy sheep farmer.

"Yes, ruined. His stock left to wander in the bush, his farm manager hand in glove with Howarth, who's a villain if ever I saw one. Dennis may be a dear but he's hopeless as a farmer, and I'd tell him so myself if I thought it would do any good. Oh, Tessa, one little day! What can we do in one little day?"

"Nothing," said Tessa with flat certainty.

Jan sat up in bed, her eyes glowing. "But of course!" she exclaimed. "Look, Tessa, Colin knows what Princess looks like. He's seen her close up, he told me so himself. And he told me that Cinnamon's mother couldn't have been far from where you found Cinnamon when she died because Cinnamon was too young to wander far alone. So all we have to do is go out there and find the body of the cow. And if it's Princess we tell Dennis, drag him out there to see with his own eyes if we must. Then he'll know Young Pat's a rogue. So that's everything solved, Cinnamon's owner found, Dennis warned about Young Pat, all the mysteries solved and I can go home in peace."

And Cinnamon would have to go to Riverlea, thought Tessa. But it would be a relief to know. And she could not help dreaming that Mr. Sanderson, who was rich and talked so kindly of her rescue of Cinnamon might . . . But he had said, "I wish she were mine." Tessa wished tomorrow were over or would never come.

ELEVEN

Cinnamon's Mother

"What do we do now?" asked Ruth, and they all looked at Jan, who was meant to be their leader.

It was nine in the morning, and they had already reached the swimming hole. A lumpy knapsack was slung from Colin's shoulder, containing a picnic lunch that the two older girls had prepared while Tessa was feeding Cinnamon. They had all day to solve the mystery of Cinnamon's mother, but they had promised not to stray into the bush.

Jan stood on the riverbank and gazed into the still, brown water. The deep pool under the shade of tall and closely growing trees looked like the visible form of all mysteries, but it held no solutions. "But, Tessa, you were farther into the bush when you saw the cow," she said. "How did you manage?"

Tessa, as if she had not heard, picked a kawakawa leaf and rubbed it between her hands. She sniffed at its peppery smell.

"Yes, how did you, Tessa?" asked Ruth.

"Well," she said unwillingly, for she had told nobody of her attempt to get lost, which now seemed so foolish that she could hardly believe it herself. "Well, I sort of started off along the riverbank. . . ."

"That's it!" said Jan, sparing her the confession. "*That* we can explore. We can't get lost beside the river, can we, Colin?"

While Colin stammered and tried to put into words the

difficult task of disagreeing with Jan, she was already pushing through the undergrowth at the water's edge.

It was not an easy journey, as Tessa already knew, but
Jan's determination forced her on and the others had no
choice but to follow, if only because none of them wanted
to greet Aunt Helen with the news that her daughter had
last been seen following a swift river into a range of bush-
covered hills.

When the undergrowth allowed, they pushed along the
bank, at other times they waded along the river itself.
Tessa had a hole in the ankle of her boot through which
the water trickled until her sock was an icy rag. When
the riverbank turned to the ooze of black mud opposite the
cave where Nutmeg had been found, the hole let that in,
too. It was not pleasant.

"Footprints," said Jan at last.

Tessa looked at the thick mud. Something had certainly
made deep imprints, but they were shapeless and half
full of water now. Colin went close to inspect them.

"Now look what you've done!" Jan almost shouted at
him. "Walking all over them with your big feet! What
sort of detective do you call yourself?"

Colin, who had never called himself any sort of detective, gave her a heartbroken look. He plodded out of the
mud and disappeared into the bush.

Jan bent over the footprints. "And now I just don't
know," she complained. "Somebody's walked here with
big feet, but I can't remember where Colin went. They
could all be his."

Tessa and Ruth looked blank. They were supposed to
be searching for a cow, not a man.

"Hey!" called Colin from among the trees. "Hey, Jan,
come and see this!"

If it had been bad detecting to walk through a few footprints, Tessa could not imagine what Jan would say to the state of the grove of pungas in which a few minutes later she found Colin. He might have been fighting a dozen enemies or perhaps practicing ballroom dancing. Clumps of moss, scraped from the ground, lay upside down around him, the tops of fern fronds hung at sharp angles to their broken ribs or were trampled into the clay, a rotten tree trunk showed pale chips where it had been recently kicked.

"But I didn't, Jan, fair dinkum I didn't. Look, there's my only footprint." Colin pointed to one among many on the trampled ground.

Jan sat down on a rotten tree trunk. "Well," she said, "this is it."

"What's what?" asked Ruth, coming out of the under-growth. "What happened? Do you think it was wild pigs?"

They all looked at her in distress. They had not thought of a solution so simple and so irrelevant. It was Colin who pointed to the clear imprint of a man-sized sole and asked with a rare flicker of imagination, "Pigs in boots? And it weren't me, Jan. Cross me 'art, it weren't."

"Very well then," said Jan from her tree trunk, "so it was a man. Now, you people live here. Do you know any reason why a man should be out in the bush?"

"Pig shooting," said Ruth at once. "This pig crashed about when they shot it and you can see where they dragged it down to the river. There's even a tuft of its hair caught on this lawyer here." She pulled a clump of sandy hair from the prickly trailer of a bush lawyer and held it out to Jan.

Jan after a brief inspection passed it to Colin. "Pig bristle?" she asked as if she had caught his own brevity of speech.

"Naw, cow."

"Riverlea Princess?"

"Dunno."

"I'm sure Sherlock Holmes would be able to tell from a big clump of hair like that."

"He a dairy farmer?"

"Oh, Colin, you are an ignoramus!"

The words were not unkindly spoken but Colin's jaw sagged in dismay. "Pity you didn't bring your friend What's-it Holmes instead of me," he said miserably. "I'm no use."

Tessa, who knew that Sherlock Holmes had lived long ago and then only in stories, began to laugh, but Jan repented and said, "You've done all the detective work so far, you and Ruth. So what now, my dear Holmes? What do you deduce from the evidence so far?"

Colin brightened at the praise, but Jan's language was too difficult for him. "Don't know how to juice," he said, "but I reckon they musta thrown her in the river."

"Threw Cinnamon's mother in the river?" Tessa could not share her horror with them because they had not seen the beauty of the honey-gold cow in life. She looked at the broken ferns and kicked-up clay. Half a dozen men perhaps, dragging something big and lifeless, branches tearing at the glowing coat, of which Colin now held a dead, discarded tuft. It was such an unnecessary insult to add to a cruel death.

"Threw her in the river?" Jan's voice had scorn enough to wither Colin.

Ruth, however, supported him with assurance. "I came through this way," she said, "while you were pushing through all the undergrowth. It's easy. Somebody might have bulldozed a path. I suppose you might really call it cowdozed."

Jan was at once on her way, with Colin and Tessa faithfully at her heels. There was a track carved through the bush and more than one tuft of cow hair to show the unpleasant manner in which it had been made.

Jan jumped from the bank and squelched beyond the tops of her boots in mud. When Colin and Ruth had each taken an arm and hauled her out, there was mud all over her and over them and one boot had disappeared beneath a mass of gurgling mud. "Leave it, Colin," she said as he reached up to his shoulder in the mud. She sat down on the bank, pulled off her other boot, pushed her muddy socks into its toe and rolled up the legs of her jeans. "That's better," she said, squelching with bare feet into the mud. "Now, let's see what we can find out about those men and their cow. Look, they dragged her down the bank here, upstream of this awful mud. Colin, stop making footprints. You're confusing me."

The water ran shallow, bouncing over the stones with an edge of white spray. It was Colin who pointed out as he bent to wash mud from the sleeve of his shirt that it was too shallow to hide a full-grown Jersey cow. "They musta been crazy to try," he said. "All that work for nothing!"

"But it wasn't for nothing," Jan said. "The cow's gone. They didn't take her up the other side or we'd see the tracks. So what did they do with her? If only we had some idea why they came out here after a dead cow in the first place we might have a chance of guessing what they did with her."

"*We* came out here after a dead cow," said Ruth.

"That's it!" Jan startled them by shouting. "Only we came to see a cow, not to spirit it away. Don't you see?" she cried impatiently at their blank faces. "There is something special about this cow; there must be. They must have got together a regular search party, brought

them all out here and searched the bush until they found
her and then dragged her down the river. Just imagine!"
Her brown eyes shone in her muddy face. "Already hidden
out in the bush where only a real, organized search could
find her, and even that isn't safe enough. They have to
drag her down to the river. And then?"

"Drag her downstream to a deeper place," said Ruth.

"They must. Yes, they must have, Ruth. Come on to a
deeper place." Jan plunged with bare feet into the mud
and with boots squelching at every step they followed.

There was no deep water before the swimming hole.
They stood at last on its bank and looked into the still
water and every stone or submerged log looked to somebody like part of a cow. Tessa thought that she would
never dare swim there again for fear of what her bare feet
might discover.

"Well that's it," said Jan, her mood plunging from
elation to despondency.

"You'd need a frogman," Colin discouragingly agreed.
"Aren't it lunchtime yet?"

Somehow, to eat lunch here, where they often took sandwiches in summer when they went swimming, seemed as
inappropriate as picnicking in a graveyard. Without discussing it, they moved on downstream toward the shallow
water below the pool, which could hide no secrets.

Between the Duggan and Howarth farms a rusty strand
of barbed wire hung low across the river, marking a boundary that had perhaps been meaningful long ago when
earlier Howarths and Duggans had planned to clear the
bush. Nobody had taken it seriously for years, and through
the trees Tessa could see where the remainder of the
fence broke off in a coil of wire.

Jan waded out into midstream, where the water rose

high on her rolled-up jeans. She pulled something from the fence and waved it high above her head as she waded back to shore.

"Jan, you're sopping. You'll have to go home," said Ruth in her most motherly tone.

"I don't care, I don't care!" sang Jan. "Our first clue in hours! Look!" She opened her clenched hand to reveal a damp shred of cow hair. Suddenly she sat down on a fallen tree trunk. "Let's eat, Colin. I'm famished."

Colin with unusual bravado insisted on eating his lunch on the far side of the fence. Ted Howarth would be furious, he pointed out, to find him not only trespassing but calmly eating sandwiches. But, since it was unlikely that Ted Howarth would be wandering in the bush, all he achieved was the inconvenience of Tessa and Ruth, who had continually to interrupt their own lunch to pass sandwiches across the fence. He might have starved for all Jan cared, who, after one scornful glance, got on with her own lunch.

Ted Howarth did not come to test Colin's courage. They finished their lunch and returned to the water, which seemed colder for the new warmth of their feet.

The afternoon passed and Ruth grew fidgety. She was disheveled enough, but Jan was scarcely visible beneath her coating of mud. They had started out with Jan's watch to guide them, but river water or mud or just bad luck had left it permanently recording half past eleven.

"Helen will just have to wait," said Jan carelessly, "if we are late, but of course we won't be." Somehow her carelessness made Ruth's perfectly reasonable concern sound like fussiness.

It was with a mixture of relief and apprehension that they at last stood before a fence in little better repair than the one across the river and saw beyond it a green paddock through which the river flowed between banks of gorse that was just coming into flower.

"Well, this is it," said Jan as she climbed between the slack and rusty strands of barbed wire. "This is Ted Howarth's land, isn't it, Colin?"

"With that gorse, who else?"

"And there," said Jan, "is the cow, or my name's not Sherlock Holmes."

There was no sign of a cow, living or dead, but they ran after her across the rough pasture. It was good to be on grass again after the long walk through cold water.

Jan ran to a space beside the river where for some reason the gorse had not flourished and grass grew to the water's edge. Or rather, grass had grown there, for now most of the small clearing was filled with dug-up soil. The digging was recent. The lumps of earth were raw and unweathered and the shovel that someone had left behind had not rusted.

Jan picked up the shovel and handed it to Colin. "Dig," she said.

Colin's eyebrows shot up, asking a question above eyes that were round with wonder, but he did not give voice to it. He took the shovel and began to dig.

"What's that awful smell?" asked Ruth.

Tessa sniffed and caught the first whiff of early gorse which, noxious pest though it might be, smelled of heaven. But there was something else, less penetrating but distinctly unpleasant. Jan looked as relaxed as her favorite Sherlock Holmes when he alone knew the solution of a mystery. Tessa felt that any questions would receive only a casual "Elementary, my dear Tessa." But the smell seemed to grow worse.

"Well, there she is." Colin leaned on his shovel and looked into the hole he had dug. Then, as the three girls moved forward, he began rapidly to shovel the earth back again.

Tessa was just in time to see a hoof before it disappeared under a shower of earth and stones. She wished she had not seen that or realized where the disgusting smell was coming from.

"You all right, Tessa?" Ruth's arm was around her shoulder. Ruth could be comforting at times.

Tessa nodded, out of gratitude to Ruth, but she was not all right. Since that one brief meeting she had loved the memory of the honey-gold cow who had been Cinnamon's mother. Now she had seen the end of the story and could scarcely listen, as they walked homeward, to Jan's enthusiastic chatter and questioning of Colin. Whether the cow was called Riverlea Princess or another name or none at all—she had been beautiful in life and was now repulsively dead. She had been Cinnamon's mother.

A car stood at the Duggans' gate and beside it, talking to Mum, was a woman so tiny and elegant that she could only be Aunt Helen.

"Oh dear," moaned Ruth, "Aunt Helen of all people. Whatever will she think of us? What will she think of you, Jan, the state you're in?"

Jan laughed and ran forward along the grass, giving a little hop every few steps as her bare feet touched a thistle or a trailing blackberry shoot. There were streaks of blood now among the mud on her legs.

"What a disgusting sight!" Aunt Helen pushed her daughter away at arm's length. "My dear child, I know society women do indulge in mud packs for their complexions, but isn't this going a little too far? Jean, dear, may we trespass on your bathroom before I pack these creatures from the wild woods into my at-present hygienic car?"

Mum, as embarrassed by the girls' appearance as Ruth herself, waved them with flustered hands toward the house and bathroom. "They haven't been like this all the holidays, Helen. I don't know what you'll think of me for letting them, but . . . Tessa, what have you been doing to that poor child?"

"If I know my daughter," laughed Aunt Helen, "it's more likely to be a case of what the 'poor child' has been doing to them. Isn't that so, Tessa? And now take me to see these remarkable orphans of yours. The only letter my daughter condescended to write me was full of nothing but Cinnamon and Nutmeg and the way you two had cared for them, especially Colin. Jan seemed to think that Colin had been wonderful."

If Aunt Helen had presented him with a fortune, Colin could not have looked more pleased or more embarrassed. He rubbed one boot against the leg of the other, nearly overbalanced and muttered something that sounded like "Aw, heck."

Tessa looked with concern at Aunt Helen's shoes. They were solid and flat-heeled, but definitely not up to the mud in the orchard.

Aunt Helen caught the direction of her glance. "I was up to my eyebrows in Taranaki mud long before you were born," she said, "though I didn't quite wallow in it as a certain member of my family seems to. Lead on."

With unexpected firmness, Mum led an eager Ruth and a meek Jan off to the house to clean up. Colin mumbled something and stumped away, so Tessa found herself alone with Aunt Helen, leading the way to the orchard. Still concerned with Ruth's picture of a town-dwelling, elegant Aunt Helen who hated to visit a farm, she tried to keep clear of the worst patches of mud, but soon Aunt Helen's shoes were thick with it and her stockings spattered. Worse still, when she was absorbed in her first sight of Cinnamon, one foot strayed into a fresh cow pat. She wiped it carelessly on a clump of grass and said, "She's a credit to you, Tessa. The shine on her coat! Oh, and here's little Nutmeg."

As Nutmeg pushed up to her, Aunt Helen squatted down to hug her. Nutmeg enjoyed a little fondling and then bounded off toward Cinnamon, challenging her to a game. Cinnamon leaped stiffly, more like a kid than a calf, and ran off with a catch-me-if-you-can look at Nutmeg.

Aunt Helen turned a laughing face up to Tessa. She looked absurdly young, far too young to be Jan's mother, as Jan herself so often looked much younger than her age. "They're adorable," she said. "And they're all yours, are they, you lucky girl?"

"Unless we find Cinnamon's owner. That's what we've been doing today, detecting a lost cow."

To her surprise, Tessa found that it was easy to tell Aunt Helen everything, even the horror of the honey-gold cow's fate that she had thought she could never share. Soon Aunt Helen knew more of the story than anyone but the four detectives and more of Tessa's feelings than she understood herself.

"Dennis Sanderson's a fool," was her verdict.

"Jan says he's clever and she's clever enough to know."

"He's a clever fool then."

Jan came out to them looking very much like the clean and well-dressed girl they had met at the bus stop, except

that her shoes were growing almost as muddy as Aunt
Helen's. Ruth preserved hers by swinging on the gate and
waiting for them to come to her.

Jan looked at her mother's shoes and stockings. "Who's
disreputable now?" she asked.

"What have you done with those awful clothes? Not
deposited them in my clean car, I hope?"

"Auntie Jean's washing them and keeping them for
when I come again. I can, can't I, Helen? She says we
could both come for Christmas if we've nothing better to
do, but I think she's too scared of you to ask you yourself. I
must know what happens to Cinnamon, and Dennis Sanderson and I are three games each. I can't bear it and
neither can he. He says his reputation as a chess player's
at stake."

"Pity he doesn't think a bit more about his reputation as
a farmer."

Jan looked at her mother. She seemed as surprised as
Tessa at the anger of her tone.

"One thing's certain," said Aunt Helen. "If Cinnamon
is his, I hope he never finds out. Tessa deserves the animal a lot more than a man who doesn't even take the
trouble to count his own stock."

"Those aren't very honest views to put into a young
girl's head," said Jan. "I want to see justice done if those
two men have cost Dennis his most valuable cow."

"Dennis! Who gave you permission to call him Dennis?
He's old enough to be your father."

"He did, and Helen dear, you're old enough to be my
mother but I call you Helen, Helen dear."

Tessa listened with amazement. She would never have
dared speak to either of her parents like that. But Aunt
Helen showed no disapproval. She argued back, "You've
known *me* for more than a fortnight, Jan dear."

"Isn't my mother's old fiancé almost part of the family?"

"He told you that?"

"I detected it. I'm quite the sleuth these days. He's still pretty gone on you, you know. I think that's why he's never married."

"Romantic little idiot!"

"He was very interested to hear you were in Manurima when I spoke to him on the phone just now."

"You spoke to him on the phone just now?"

"I had to tell him that we'd found Princess."

"Oh, and what did your dear friend Dennis say to that?"

"Like a responsible farmer he'll check up with Young Pat—insist he sees Princess with his own eyes and if she isn't there—well, I wouldn't like to be in Young Pat's shoes."

"Fair enough," Aunt Helen admitted, "if Young Pat's honest, which I doubt." She turned to Tessa. "You'll have to keep an eye on that man now. Make sure he does insist on seeing Princess. And if he starts talking any lawyer's talk about his rights to your calf, you stand up for your own rights, which may not be in any of Dennis Sanderson's law books but are obvious to anyone with a bit of human feeling. If he wants Cinnamon you tell him he can come and take her by force."

"Yes, Aunt Helen," said Tessa, unsure whether to laugh or be frightened.

"And if I come at Christmas and find Cinnamon at Riverlea, the Waipuke will flow red with Dennis Sanderson's blood."

Jan, unperturbed by her mother's bloodthirstiness, asked, "We will come at Christmas?"

"Of course. Do you think I'd leave my niece's happiness in Dennis Sanderson's hands without dropping in to see if he needs murdering? Besides, I like it here."

Jan laughed and Tessa began to laugh too. It was good to have an ally as determined as Aunt Helen, even if she did have a rather alarming way of expressing her concern. And it would be good to have them both at Christmas. She only wished that Aunt Helen hated Mr. Sanderson less. She guessed Jan's dream, and if Mr. Sanderson wanted a wife, Aunt Helen would have been a great improvement on Jenny Wren. And it would be fun to have Jan at Riverlea all through the holidays. But Aunt Helen's last words as she drove off with the two clean girls and their luggage were, "Remember, Tessa—justice or revenge! Don't let that man Sanderson rob you!"

TWELVE

Jenny Wren's Livestock Show

There were two days of fear before Mr. Sanderson telephoned and then Tessa was so nervous that she could hardly understand what he was saying. "Safe and sound with a fine heifer calf," she heard at last and she realized that he was talking about Riverlea Princess.

"Then who?" she stammered. "But all the men admired her. Who? What?" She was relieved and disappointed all at once. She had been proud to think of Riverlea Princess as Cinnamon's mother, but she wanted Cinnamon to be her own.

"I know, Tessa. I find it hard to believe that so many sober dairy farmers could be wrong and that Cinnamon's just the daughter of some miserable animal that her owner didn't find worth claiming. I wonder. There's something we had in mind, Jennifer—Miss Renfrew—and I, that could throw light on this, at least establish that Cinnamon is well bred. But that, if it comes to anything, won't be till the end of term. So until then you can just sit back and enjoy Cinnamon's company. Everything's been done that anyone can do to find her owner. Relax, Tessa. She's your calf now."

Cinnamon certainly felt like Tessa's calf and she did relax, only wondering at times about the mysterious something at the end of term. It did not really trouble her whether or not Cinnamon was entitled to a pedigree— Cinnamon was a sweet-natured animal and her friend. But uncertainty remained while so many farmers judged the calf well bred and yet nobody claimed her.

At first she was surprised that Jenny Wren could be involved in anything to do with farming, but there was a change that term at Manurima School. A new subject called "rural studies" made its appearance.

The children of Manurima, well versed in the gossip of adults, knew the reason for that. Mr. Sanderson believed in rural education for rural children and Jenny Wren liked to please Mr. Sanderson. They were grateful to him. Nothing in their lives compared with the hilarity of being taught farming by Jenny Wren. Wednesday afternoon, rural-studies afternoon, meant two hours of barely concealed laughter while they competed at finding questions to trip Jenny Wren in her carefully prepared lessons or wondered at her ignorance of things they had known all their lives.

But the subject was not all laughter. Once they visited the Hopes' farm, where as dairy-farm children they were at home and full of the curiosity that Jenny Wren found lacking in the classroom. Later, near the end of the term, the school bus took them all to Riverlea, where Young Pat, a lively and entertaining teacher, instructed them in the less familiar work of the sheep farm. And at the end of their visit Mr. Sanderson joined them to announce the plans that he and Miss Renfrew had made for an End-of-Term Livestock Show.

Many of the children had calves they had raised themselves, some had ponies, and most had a pet of some sort. They would be judged by an expert from many miles away who had often judged the Jersey sections at livestock shows, and there would be ribbons and rosettes and, to Tessa's delight and the disappointment of the Howarths and their friends, book token prizes.

Tessa went home elated. Without a pedigree, Cinnamon could never be entered in a regular livestock show.

but here at least was a chance for her to be judged by a real judge. Mr. Sanderson had been right. Cinnamon's fine breeding would be established by the praise of an expert and yet, since nobody had claimed her, she would still be Tessa's calf. Things could not have worked out better for Tessa and Cinnamon. For Nutmeg there would be the pets' section and, although Tessa was less sure of the chances of a wild goat against more normal pets, she dreamed of glory for both her friends.

The day of the show, the last Saturday of term, came slowly but it came at last. Excitement had spread beyond the school. The farmers left their work and put on clean shirts with collars and ties in honor of Mr. Maskell, the show judge. Many of their wives had been at school all morning setting up trestle tables and making sandwiches. Whatever the occasion, people had to be fed, and fed well, in Manurima.

The children arrived riding ponies or leading calves that shone after a morning's hard work with brush and comb. There were young lambs with ribbons around their necks and ponies with braided manes; there was a bantam hen with a family of ducklings in a cardboard box, a hedgehog, two guinea pigs, a variety of dogs, and a fat and stubborn sheep that several years ago had been the Hope twins' pet lamb. But, because it was dairying country and the children were involved with the work of the farms, more than anything there were calves, each of them guaranteed by the owner's parents to have been reared by the child alone.

Tessa's hopes fell as she lined up Cinnamon with the row of glossy calves. She had not doubted until then that Cinnamon would win, but the other calves looked so beautiful, so sleek and well groomed. Suppose the judge

recognized Cinnamon at once as just a scruffy stray from
the bush? Behind them Nutmeg strained at a piece of
twine and bleated. Cinnamon turned around and pulled at
her halter and bellowed unhappily for her friend, while
the other calves obediently stood at their owners' sides.
Mr. Maskell, not knowing of the friendship, would just
see an ill-trained calf, unfit for the show ring.

He moved from one calf to another, examining it and
making notes in a little book. He spent a long time looking at a fine, perfectly mannered animal of Gregory Hope;
the Hope brothers' stock was second only to the Riverlea
herd among the herds of the Manurima district. Then he
came to Tessa. He looked sternly at her and not at
Cinnamon. Tessa was sure he was about to disqualify
them for Cinnamon's bad behavior.

"It's Nutmeg," she tried to explain. "Nutmeg will bleat
and upset her."

Mr. Maskell turned to Mr. Sanderson, who as organizer
of the show was following behind him, ready to give any
help that was needed. "I understood this class was for
calves reared by the children themselves," he said.

"That's right," said Mr. Sanderson, looking as puzzled
as Tessa herself.

"Then how did this one get in?"

"Cinnamon? But she's the most child-reared calf in the
district. You must get Tessa to tell you the story later.
This is the one calf I can personally guarantee to have
been raised without parental help."

Mr. Maskell looked as hard at Tessa as if he had come to
judge her and not the calf. "Tell me," he said to Mr.
Sanderson, "is her father a millionaire or a madman or
both?"

"Neither that I know of," said Mr. Sanderson, smiling
toward Dad's long scarecrow form as he tugged at Nut-

meg's rope until his sleeves were halfway up his arms. "Why should he be?"

The judge gave him a pitying look. "You're a sheep man, of course," he said. "Your late brother would have understood. These others"—he looked along the line of calves—"are nice enough animals, the calves I'd expect in a children's show. But this animal—well, I just didn't expect to find anything like this out here—outside Riverlea, that is. Still, if you guarantee her, Mr. Sanderson, I'll have to accept that her father has a great deal of faith in his daughter. Justified, I must say, except for the calf's training. That sort of behavior wouldn't do in the show ring, I'm afraid."

"Joe," Mr. Sanderson called, "can't you bring that goat around here where Cinnamon can see her? Can't you see the poor creature's going out of her mind with worry?"

Dad slouched self-consciously to the front of the row of calves, dragging Nutmeg, whose one idea was to be right beside her friend. Cinnamon, however, was content with only the sight of Nutmeg and stood as perfectly for the judge as she had during their many rehearsals in the orchard.

"That's better," said Mr. Maskell, "if somewhat unorthodox." And without further examination of Cinnamon and without writing a word in his notebook he passed on to the next calf. Mr. Sanderson, as he followed, winked at Tessa.

Mrs. Maskell judged the pets' section. She seemed less interested in looking at the animals than in questioning their owners. Did they find time to feed their pets themselves? Did they take their dogs for walks every day? She had left many blushing pet owners behind when she came to Tessa. "Now, here's a pet who can feed and exercise herself," she said, smiling at Nutmeg.

"Oh, no," protested little Patsy Hope, who stood beside Tessa, tugging with her twin sister at the rope of the former pet lamb.

"No?" Mrs. Maskell smiled.

"Not when she was little," explained the talkative Patsy, "because Mr. Howarth shot her mother and Tessa fed her like me and Sharon fed Lucy here, pretending that we were mother sheep, only she was a mother goat. Otherwise Nutmeg would have died in the bush, you see, and my father says Ted Howarth didn't care."

"I see," said Mrs. Maskell and moved on to a family of bantam chickens.

Before she announced the prizewinners' names, Mrs. Maskell made a little speech about the care of pets and about children who begged for a pet and, as soon as the novelty wore off, left all the responsibility to their parents. "Judging children's pets is always difficult," she said. "How can you compare a guinea pig with a sheepdog and a wild goat? So perhaps I've judged the pet owners as much as their pets. And I have no doubts as to where the first prize should go. Nutmeg has had her troubles." She had been making inquiries, apparently, for she looked straight at Ted Howarth. "But she found a friend in need. She's a beautiful animal and she is a child's pet, not a child's amusement and a parent's responsibility."

Her husband was content to give the prizes without a lecture. He simply announced, "First Tessa Duggan's Cinnamon, second Gregory Hope's Buttercup."

With red ribbons around their necks and red rosettes pinned to their halters, Cinnamon and Nutmeg were tied side by side to the school fence while Tessa, with two book tokens clutched in her hand and her face hot with pride and embarrassment, followed Mr. and Mrs. Maskell and Mr. Sanderson into the school for afternoon tea. They

sat at a special table with a white tablecloth at one end of
the room while everybody else helped themselves from
the trestle tables and ate standing up. Through the window she could see the crowd around Cinnamon and Nutmeg, who sat in the shade of the fence, back to back, as
content with each other's company as, in a time unimag-
inably distant, the two little orphans in the bush had been.
She turned unwillingly away from them to answer Mr.
and Mrs. Maskell's questions about the finding and rearing of Cinnamon.

Suddenly there was a commotion behind her. She
turned to see Billy Howarth running down the room with
a red ribbon in one hand and a red rosette in the other.
"They're mine! They're mine!" he shouted. "Her stole
Dad's calf and them's Dad's prizes."

Warren, lumbering behind and shouting even louder,
just caught up with him as he reached the little table
where Tessa and Mr. Sanderson and Mr. and Mrs. Maskell
sat staring. "Give those here, Billy," he said.

"Them's mine. You said, Warren. Them's our Dad's."

"Did you tell him that, Warren?" asked Mr. Sanderson.

"Yeah, sure."

"You told him that Cinnamon was your father's calf?"

"Sure," said Warren virtuously. "A man can only tell
the truth. But you listen here, you daft kid," he told
Billy, seizing his shoulder with a rough hand. "Y'know
Dad don't want us tellin'. Y'know he said like Tessa saved
the little calf's life and we don't have no right to claim
what was ours because all we did was lose her mother."

"That doesn't sound like Ted Howarth to me," remarked Mr. Sanderson.

"Ted Howarth!" repeated Mrs. Maskell. "You mean that
lovely little calf belongs to the man who goes around
shooting nursing mothers?"

"My dad don't . . ." began Warren, but Mr. Sanderson
interrupted with, "Warren, I think we'd better hear
about this from your father himself." As Warren slouched
off leading Billy, whose hand still clutched the now grimy
rosette, he said, "It's all right, Tessa. I don't know what
this little performance is in aid of, but Ted Howarth isn't
getting that calf by turning his sons into a bad comedy
act. Consider me hired as lawyer for the defense." He
smiled, but Tessa could not smile back.

They waited with tea growing cold and cakes and sandwiches untouched for, so it seemed to Tessa, a very long
time. Once Mrs. Maskell with a friendly smile offered her
a plate of cream cakes. Too shy to refuse, she took one
and left it, forgotten, on her plate.

At last the two boys returned, followed by their father
and Young Pat.

"Hear my young Billy's been telling tales out of school,"
said Mr. Howarth amiably, standing beside the table with
his booted legs spread wide and his old felt hat pushed to
the back of his head. "Not all there, isn't Billy."

Young Pat, fresh and smiling and well dressed, stepped
forward to his friend's side. "Now, look here, Ted, don't
be a sentimental fool."

Mr. Sanderson raised one eyebrow and Tessa, catching
the expression on his face, held back a giggle. It was the
most solemn moment of her life, but the thought of Mr.
Howarth as sentimental was so absurd and Mr. Sanderson's silent comment made it into a private joke between
them.

"Fair's fair," said Mr. Howarth. "Farming's a gamble
and I lost. Why should I rob the child of a calf she's reared
so lovingly? I loved that cow like me own child but she's
dead and buried. That's a farmer's life and a man learns

to accept it, the rough with the smooth, even if it's precious little smooth for a poor cow farmer with a wife and six kids to feed."

He took out a rather gray handkerchief and loudly blew his nose. That was too much for Mr. Sanderson: he roared with laughter. "All this talent wasted!" he said. "We really must start a drama society. I congratulate you on your performance, Ted, and on your sons'. Of Pat's Thespian talents I was already aware. Now, do you think we can call an end to the performance and get on with our tea?"

"Oh, very clever, Mr. Sanderson. I told you, Pat, I told you what'd be the way of it, them with their educations and long words against a poor cow farmer what's only got his rights and the love and care what he gave his cow. I told you just honesty and love wasn't no use in this world."

"Come off it, Ted." Mr. Sanderson's laughter had died and his voice was stern. "We're going to be impressed by facts, not by noble speeches. Your sons have stated and you imply, if I correctly interpret your heroic meanderings, that you are the rightful owner of Cinnamon. All I'm asking, man, is that either you give us a little proof or that you leave us in peace."

"Proof, sure I got proof." Mr. Howarth gave a questioning, even a nervous, glance toward Young Pat.

"He's got proof," said Young Pat confidently. "But where's your humanity, Mr. Sanderson? Can't you see the poor man's overwrought? He loved that cow, that I can vouch for. I was with him when he found her poor dead body. Nothing would do for him but to drag her all the way out of the bush and bury her on his own land, as near as he could to give a poor dumb beast Christian burial."

A whoop of laughter came from the gathering crowd behind Tessa. She turned to see grins on many faces and her cousin Trevor with heaving shoulders clutching for support at Bernie Hope. The men had no doubts in their opinion of a tenderhearted Ted Howarth who gave "Christian burial" to a favorite cow. But Tessa had seen the grave. She had followed the arduous journey down the river.

"There is a grave," she said desperately.

"So at last we have one fact," said Mr. Sanderson. "One dead cow buried. It's a long way from your claim to ownership of Cinnamon."

"I'm not making no . . ."

"Of course you are, Ted," Young Pat interrupted, putting his hand on Mr. Howarth's shoulder. "I've told you before, you're your own worst enemy. The story's out now and we may as well see this through and claim your own valuable property. She is valuable, isn't she?" he asked Mr. Maskell.

Mr. Maskell took a moment to find his voice. He was evidently not used to such dramatic sequels to his judging. He cleared his throat. "Unregistered stock," he said cautiously. "No pedigree. Yes, she's valuable to any man with an eye for good stock, though not, of course, as valuable as if we had proof of her parentage."

"But we have proof." Young Pat paused to look with satisfaction at the sensation he had created, both at the table and among the watching farmers. Nobody laughed now. "We have her mother's papers and her father's, we've all that's required to register her as Riverlea Cinnamon, daughter of Riverlea Princess."

It was a dramatic moment and Young Pat, having worked up to it, savored it like an actor at the climax of a play. He seemed almost to be waiting for applause. But instead there was a dead silence, equally a tribute to his sense of drama.

Mr. Sanderson broke it with a cold, precise voice, exchanging for the emotion of the stage the logic of the courtroom: "So Ted Howarth is the owner of Riverlea Princess?"

"As usual you've hit the nail right on the head, Mr. Sanderson," Young Pat told him approvingly. "Last year Ted had a rare bit of luck. Ten dollars, wasn't it, Ted, you'd put on a rank outsider at Trentham. Instead of having a good time, like a lot of men would, Ted looks around straight away for a way to improve his farm, decides on a really good piece of stock, makes your brother a good offer for Princess, and your brother accepts."

"And never bothers to tell a soul about it," came Trevor's voice. "All in the day's work for Mr. Edward Howarth, the distinguished cattle breeder."

Young Pat turned on him, his blue eyes sharp with indignation. "Tell you and be faced with nasty little jokes like that one? When have any of his neighbors ever made Ted feel like confiding in them? When have they ever suggested but that he and his poor farm were a joke? Wouldn't you have laughed at the idea of him trying to better himself? Why—"

"That's enough, Pat," Mr. Sanderson broke in. "We've got the message and we accept that Ted's sensitive soul couldn't bear the scorn of his neighbors. Just one thing, Pat—how come that you showed me Riverlea Princess alive and well a month or more after Ted's cow had died?"

Young Pat for the first time looked slightly abashed. "I confess a small deception, Mr. Sanderson," he said in his frankest manner. "Like I said, Ted being unwilling to become a laughingstock for his ambition, I thought it best to go along with him, poor Princess being in her

grave by then and nobody's property, you might say. I
showed you Riverlea Sheba, a fine animal, as Mr. Maskell
here will testify."

Mr. Maskell nodded. "I remember Sheba well," he said,
"a fine cow, though not the equal of Riverlea Princess."
He looked searchingly at Mr. Sanderson's face as if he
might discover there an indication as to how the man who
owned them could mistake one pedigree Jersey for another. There was a scornful murmur among the farmers.
It was a point for Young Pat.

"Well," said Mr. Sanderson, a spark of anger sharpen-
ing his voice, "there's one way to settle this. You have
papers to prove your story? Then you won't mind showing them to Mr. Maskell and myself?"

If he had meant to call their bluff, it was a failure.
"Right away," said Young Pat airily. "Come on, Ted."

As they left the room, there was an expression on Ted
Howarth's face that Tessa couldn't quite describe to herself. There was triumph and there was guile and there
was something else that frightened her. Mr. Howarth was
sure he was going to win.

The adults of the party left their unfinished tea and
went out to look at Cinnamon. As she rose to follow them,
Tessa felt Mr. Sanderson's hand on her shoulder and heard
his voice say as if through a dream, "Don't worry, Tessa.
They're bluffing. They'll never prove a tissue of lies like
that. Didn't I say I was hired as lawyer for the defense?"

Tessa tried to smile at him but her face was too stiff
to move. She followed him, shivering, into the cloudless
summer afternoon.

She hung back from the crowd that had gathered
around Cinnamon, putting the broad shoulders of several
farmers between herself and the soft brown eyes of her
friend. It was all her fault for wanting to show off, to

win prizes, instead of being content with the happy private days in the orchard. The book tokens in her hand were twisted into grimy corkscrews. She hated the book tokens and the soiled ribbon and rosette that somebody had taken from Billy and replaced on Cinnamon's neck.

Her father came quietly and stood beside her. His face was dark with anger, but he said nothing. When, after a very long time, Ted Howarth and Young Pat returned, he placed a hand on her shoulder and steered her away from them, through the crowd, to where her two friends were tethered to the fence. Cinnamon stretched out her neck and gave a little moo of recognition. She was unhappy tied there with a crowd of strangers pressing about her. Tessa put out a hand to comfort her and the calf sniffed it as if to make sure that this at last was the person she could trust. Tessa put an arm across her neck. Cinnamon trusted her but she felt that the trust was misplaced.

Mr. Sanderson took several official-looking sheets of paper from a large envelope that Mr. Howarth had given him. The larger ones he studied and passed on to Mr. Maskell, then returned to the envelope, but two small and flimsy pieces of paper occupied the men for a long time. Tessa could not hear what they said but she could see their frowns. Then Mr. Sanderson spent a long time talking to Ted Howarth. He was questioning him, she supposed, and making him tell the truth, which was a lawyer's job. And Mr. Sanderson was a lawyer, her lawyer for the defense. He must know how to find out the truth, unless he had lost his skill in six months of farming.

At last he left Mr. Howarth and walked slowly over to Tessa. He held out the two flimsy pieces of paper. "I'm sorry, Tessa," he said.

Tessa took the papers, because he seemed to expect her

to, but her hand was trembling and her mind was dazed;
she could not read them. Dad's hand reached across her
shoulder and took them from her. "Well, Sanderson," he
asked after a moment, "what's your answer to these?"

Mr. Sanderson's voice came through a dead silence,
strangely quiet and helpless: "No answer, Joe. Two receipts signed by my brother, one for the sale of Riverlea
Princess, one for the service of our bull, just nine-and-a-
half-months before Tessa found Cinnamon. They're genuine, Joe. The papers for Princess, the pedigree and all,
Young Pat could have taken from his own manager's office,
but these—I'm sorry, Tessa."

"Sorry?" Dad stormed. "Sorry, Mr. Lawyer Sanderson?
You promised a kid, and this is all the fight you can make
for her? Well, I'm not so easily beaten. I'll take Ted
Howarth to court, I'll hire a proper lawyer, not one who
probably played at that job like he plays at farming. I'll
make him sorry he ever tried . . ."

"Please, Dad," Tessa cried urgently. She could not stand
his anger, not on top of everything else. "Dad, you always said somebody owned Cinnamon. Now we know."
She was surprised to hear her own voice speaking so
calmly. She untied Cinnamon's rope from the fence post,
trying not to fumble too much, for her eyes were misty
and it was hard to see what she was doing. She put the
end of the rope into Mr. Howarth's hand and watched him
lead Cinnamon away. Nutmeg, seeing her friend disappear, began to bleat and strain against her rope. Tessa
patted her neck and tried to comfort her.

Something was thrust into her hand. "Here," said
Warren Howarth. "Dad says these are yours."

Tessa let the crumpled ribbon and rosette slide from
her hand. Then very slowly she trod them into the mud
beside the fence.

"Tessa!" she heard a voice say. It was Jenny Wren, of course, suddenly getting responsible for her pupil's behavior. Where had she been when Billy Howarth snatched the ribbon off another person's calf? Tessa looked her in the eye and ground the ribbon deeper into the mud. All her rage seemed to be in that foot. The rest of her was calm.

"Tessa, pick those things up!"

Tessa continued to press the ribbon into the mud. There was a grim sort of pleasure in defying Jenny Wren. She was too brimful of unhappiness to be hurt by any schoolteacher's anger. Nothing could ever hurt her again after watching Cinnamon being led away by Ted Howarth.

Mr. Sanderson said something to Jenny Wren. Tessa could not hear what he said but she knew it was a plea for herself. He dared take her side when less than half an hour ago he had promised her that Ted Howarth would not have Cinnamon! She felt the damp rags of screwed-up cardboard in her hand that had once been Mr. Sanderson's book token prizes. Carefully, one after the other, she aimed them at his face.

Nobody spoke, nobody moved, not even Jenny Wren reproached her for her rudeness. Then Dad's hand was under her elbow, steering her toward the gate. He had untied Nutmeg and she dragged ahead of them as if she too wanted to see the last of the school playground.

Or perhaps her simple and loyal little mind supposed that they were off to join Cinnamon, for, once in the back of the truck, she bleated miserably. Tessa wished that she could ride in the back to comfort her but she was too tired and unhappy to argue with Dad. Suddenly she was very tired indeed. She listened drowsily to Dad's angry voice as he made plans for teaching Ted Howarth a lesson. Over many years Ted Howarth had refused to help with either money or labor in mending the boundary fences between the two farms. Dad had been patient. But now he would take Ted Howarth to court. There was the gorse too, that ran riot on his land, its seeds a continual threat to his more responsible neighbors; that would be reported and Ted Howarth would be fined as he should have been years ago. Ted Howarth would live to regret that he had ever interfered with the Duggans and their animals.

Tessa listened. Dad meant well, but it was all so unimportant. No amount of quarreling about boundary fences and gorse would get Cinnamon back.

THIRTEEN

Aunt Helen Speaks Her Mind

Sunday passed like a bad dream for Tessa—and for
Nutmeg too, if goats have bad dreams. Nutmeg was not a
highly intelligent animal—even Tessa had to admit that.
Nor was she devoted to Tessa, as were Cinnamon and
Sam. But to the limits of her small ability she was involved
with Cinnamon, and she mourned as only a goat can with
an endless stream of heartbroken bleats that came so
loudly and unceasingly from the orchard and into the
house that Dad, his temper almost bursting him as he
struggled to keep it down for Tessa's sake, broke off his
Sunday afternoon rest to take a long, aimless walk across
the farm, and even Mum said sharply, "Can't you keep
that animal quiet?"

If Nutmeg took the separation badly, how was Cinnamon feeling, not only robbed of her friends but in a
strange paddock and surrounded by Howarths? There
was only one way to find out: on the school bus on Monday morning Tessa sat next to Billy Howarth. Billy was
surprised but not uncooperative. He answered her questions with a friendly enough grin, but all he could find to
say was "Dunno." From the seat behind, Warren listened
with a sly face that was his father's in miniature. Warren
was no fool; if he chose he could give a better answer
than "Dunno." But Tessa would not ask him and he vol-
unteered nothing. It was six-year-old Carol who finally
leaned across the aisle and said something which she made
out to be, "Him's crazy, din't ya know? And so's yer old
calf."

Next morning it was Warren who approached Tessa, almost politely, with a message from his father. What did Cinnamon eat? This was stranger still. Since she had been weaned, Cinnamon had grazed like any other calf with an occasional handful of calf nuts as a special treat. There were calf nuts in the pocket of the dress Tessa was wearing as, despite Mum's objections, there were in all her pockets. She gave them to Warren, two calf nuts in a fluff of loose threads.

Warren turned them over in his hand. "Them things won't keep her alive," he said. "Dad says she's spoiled, that's what, a kid's spoiled pet. Just stands at the gate going 'Moo,' and he reckons she don't have the gumption to feed herself. I never seen such a useless, hopeless, crazy animal in all me born days."

Warren was shorter than Tessa, but much more solidly built, and a habitual fighter while she had never used her fists before. She lashed out at him in a blind fury that was as much unhappiness as anger and as blindly met the answering whirlwind of his fists. It surprised her to see him lying crying on the ground with his arms clutching his head. She looked around to see who had hit him, but there was only a circle of openmouthed spectators and beyond them Vivienne Ritchie running toward the classroom and screaming that Tessa Duggan was murdering Warren Howarth. Jenny Wren came out, dealt with Warren's bleeding nose, and then dealt with Tessa. The things she said hurt long after Warren's tears had given place to a grin as impudent as ever.

Knocking down Warren Howarth achieved nothing. Tessa was surprised and ashamed and agreed with the worst things that Jenny Wren could say about her. She did not like Warren Howarth and part of the dislike was for his readiness with his fists, especially if his opponent was smaller than he. But Warren was a boy and meant to be rougher than a girl. Tessa hated herself as she could never have hated Warren or anybody else. She had hurt Warren and she had made herself so ashamed before the whole Howarth family that she would never be able to ask them again how Cinnamon was.

Nutmeg continued to cry. She ate little and never played. By Friday afternoon Tessa had made up her mind. Nutmeg's behavior might have been described as "crazy" by a stranger and she did not doubt that a similar misery had caused the Howarths to use that word of Cinnamon.

On Friday afternoon as soon as she got home from school, Tessa tied a rope around Nutmeg's neck and led her out of the orchard and along the road toward the Howarths' farm. Nutmeg followed meekly, her head lowered and her pace slow, as if it no longer mattered to her where she was led.

All six Howarth children were playing at the front of the house. The younger four were making mud pies and covering one another with mud while Warren and Billy were climbing on the rusty corrugated-iron roof of the front porch. Warren was the first to see Tessa and Nutmeg. "Hey, look what the wind's blown in!" he called. "Mrs. Cassius Clay and Daftie the goat!"

"Don' you 'it 'im," yelled Carol. "Dad, Dad, she's come to 'it Wa'en!"

At that all the younger Howarths set up such a shrieking that Ted Howarth himself appeared from around the side of the house. He carried a pitchfork and for a moment Tessa thought he was armed to revenge his son. But the grin with which he greeted her was almost friendly. In-

deed, a grin from Ted Howarth and not his usual scowl
was a mark of friendship that she had never before
earned.

"Been wantin' to see you," he said, leaning on the gate
with the pitchfork propped beside him. "Shut up, you
lot!" he roared at his children. It had no effect but he
went on as if satisfied: "Got a bone to pick with you, young
lady. What you been doing to my calf, eh?"

Tessa had to think. She had not touched any of Ted
Howarth's calves. Then the realization came like a cold
hand clutching her spine: "my calf" meant Cinnamon
and when she had completed her visit, Nutmeg would be
"my goat." "It's all right," she said as if it were not she
but Mr. Howarth who needed reassurance. "She'll be all
right now, Mr. Howarth. They said she was off her food
and crying. She's been pining for Nutmeg."

"Nutmeg?" he repeated as if he thought it some strange
part of the calf's diet. Then he looked at the kid and
gave a snort of laughter. "Oh, that thing! Well, she'll have
to get over that, won't she? Haven't got no time to waste
on livestock that behaves like primmer donners."

"But I've brought you Nutmeg so that they can be together. She's yours now." She held out to him the end of
Nutmeg's rope. She only wanted to get away from Ted
Howarth, scowling again, away from the mud-spattered,
screaming children and from Warren and Billy perched
on the roof and grinning like monkeys.

"What we want with an old goat?" asked Ted Howarth
and was nearly knocked over by a rush of children toward
the proffered rope. "Mine, mine," they yelled. "Saw her
first. Mine!"

Tessa screamed above the clamor, "Please, Mr. Howarth, please let her be with Cinnamon. She'll eat more,
she'll give more milk, she'll win more prizes." It was look-

ing a long way ahead and Tessa did not know what effect Nutmeg could have on Cinnamon's milk yield, but she knew that she must speak to Ted Howarth in terms of profit for himself rather than the happiness of young animals.

The rope was snatched from her hand and Nutmeg was dragged through the gate. Warren had swung down from the roof and was pushing her from the rear while his little brothers and sisters tugged at the rope.

"Don't let them, please," Tessa begged their father.

"She's our goat, see," said Warren, aiming a sharp blow at Nutmeg's hindquarters. "Gerrup, you stubborn old goat." Nutmeg in terror obeyed and goat and children disappeared around the side of the house.

Tessa looked at Mr. Howarth. That was not what she had meant. She had thought of Cinnamon and Nutmeg together in their own paddock. Even if it was Ted Howarth's paddock, they would not mind if they had each other. And now she had only given the Howarth children a new plaything. She wanted to explain, but the words would not come. Tears would have come easily, but she was not going to cry in front of Ted Howarth.

"Do what I can," he said, almost kindly. "They'll soon get tired of her." And she realized that, for all his bluster, Ted Howarth was not master in his own house. He yelled, "Stop that!" toward the noise of his children, then shrugged. "Try to make the calf happy," he muttered. Then, with a sudden friendly grin: "Wish I'd been there when you flattened that son of mine."

Tessa turned and plodded home. She had done all she could, but she had achieved nothing except to provide Nutmeg with fresh unhappiness.

Dad had the cows in and had nearly finished milking when she returned. She had forgotten that the last day of the term meant early milking and going to town to meet Ruth. Dad was not angry. He had seen the orchard gate swinging open and had guessed the reason.

"Are they happy to be together again?" he asked as they worked side by side, washing the milking-machine parts.

At the kindness in his voice the tears that Tessa had been holding back poured into the soapy water.

Dad scrubbed unnecessarily hard at the bright stainless steel and said nothing more until the job was finished and Tessa was in control of herself again. Then he asked almost shyly if she wanted to go with him to meet Ruth. At the beginning of the August holidays that invitation had begun a storm of misunderstandings. Tears burned behind Tessa's eyes as she remembered the distant times of a term ago when she had lost Dad's friendship for the sake of Cinnamon and Nutmeg.

She had his friendship now. As they drove along in the familiar intimacy of the old truck, he was at first angry with the Howarths, then sorry for Tessa, then angry again. "Look, I'll get you a proper tame goat," he offered, "a real white milking goat." He looked at her face, which was as white as any tame goat's, muttered something about Ted Howarth and then thought again. "Wasn't it a pony you always wanted? Your Uncle Alec was tellin' me about one that's going cheap. Look, how would you like Sam for your own dog? Make a pet of him, I don't mind. I'll get another pup to train as a cattle dog. Look, Tessa, there's six weeks of holiday on the farm and away from that Renfrew woman. Doesn't that make you feel better? You can work on the farm with me and Colin, never mind what Ruthie says. You're a real farmer. I'm proud of you, Tessa, fair dinkum I am, the way you brought up that calf. You're my farm boy, eh, old son?"

Tessa smiled although fresh tears were streaking her

face. And then she was ashamed. How could she be happy at being Dad's farm-boy daughter when Cinnamon and Nutmeg were suffering under the care of Ted Howarth and his brood?

Three days before Christmas Aunt Helen and Jan arrived. As soon as they had unpacked, Tessa took them out to see the little tent in the garden where she was to sleep. She had always wanted to sleep in a tent, but until the arrival of two visitors to a house with only one spare bed she had never had an excuse.

"And now," said Aunt Helen as she got to her feet after inspecting the tent, "can we visit Cinnamon and Nutmeg?"

She was at the orchard gate before Tessa could bring out her story. She stayed there, listening, with one hand on the gate, and then turned toward Tessa with a face so angry that Tessa tried in alarm to think what she had done wrong.

"That man!" said Aunt Helen. "If I meet that man, I'll give him such a piece of my mind that he'll wish he'd never been born!"

"He's a great, ignorant, dishonest bully," Jan agreed.

Aunt Helen looked surprised. "Who, Dennis Sanderson?" she asked.

"That villain Howarth."

"Oh, him." Aunt Helen wrinkled her nose as if the name of Ted Howarth offended it. "I was at school with Ted. A nasty little boy and he hasn't improved with age. But Dennis Sanderson's supposed to be an intelligent and responsible human being, not a feeble ninny."

"Helen dear," Jan protested, half laughing at her mother's anger, "it's hardly Dennis's fault if his brother sold Princess."

"Sold Princess! That's a likely story! Dennis is a fool
and Ted's a rogue. Young Pat's the only one of them with
any brains and if Dennis had a grain of sense he'd have
sacked him months ago. The man's not fit to be in charge
of a farm like Riverlea, or anything else, for that matter,
and I'll tell him so if I see him."

Tessa hoped that the meeting would never take place.
But her hopes faded next day when an invitation arrived
for the whole family and their visitors to a party at Riverlea on Christmas Eve.

Aunt Helen accepted with alarming joy. Tessa tried to
persuade Jan to argue with her mother, but Jan would not
hear of it. "Keep those two from meeting?" she asked
and, when Tessa persisted, became smug and secretive
in her best Sherlock Holmes manner.

Mum was no more useful. She was shy and flattered at
such an invitation, but, if she was nervous of going, she
was terrified of offending her rich neighbor with a refusal.

Even Dad was impressed by the invitation. The Ford
truck sparkled from its first washing in months as they
set out on Christmas Eve, proud of their appearance, but
self-conscious in best party clothes that stayed in the closet
from one year's end to the next.

Jenny Wren met them at the door of Riverlea. Standing
beside Mr. Sanderson, her face flushed by the heat of the
kitchen to the same rose pink as her nylon dress, her long
blond hair hanging forward across her cheeks, she looked,
to Tessa's alarm, as if she were already rehearsing for her
position as the young mistress of Riverlea.

She watched Aunt Helen anxiously but, instead of the
threatened attack on Mr. Sanderson, she gave a display of
good if rather chilly manners. She questioned Jenny Wren
with apparently friendly interest. Imagine being so devoted to her work that she stayed on a week beyond the

end of term! Jenny Wren uncomfortably admitted her devotion to Manurima School and muttered something about preparing work for next term. Then she hastily escaped into the kitchen where, it appeared, she had been busy all day. "She can't have prepared much work today," remarked Tessa, puzzled by this new revelation of Jenny Wren as dedicated teacher.

Ruth gave her one of her pitying adult looks. "Use your head, Tessa," she said.

Before she had used it to any purpose Tessa was caught up in the party. Everybody she knew seemed to be there —her Duggan relations and her Ritchie relations, Young Pat looking very handsome and cheerful, the Hope brothers and the three Hope children, almost every farmer in the district except the Howarths.

The children played games, the young adults danced, the older adults sat gossiping, and everybody ate more than it was really comfortable to eat. The big old house with its bright lights and spacious rooms, all so different from the bustling little farmhouses they knew, made it a strange, glittering evening, more like something Tessa had read about in a book than real life in Manurima. She would not have been surprised to look through the window and see snow on the ground like a storybook Christmas instead of full-blown roses nodding against the window. And when, after supper, Mr. Sanderson shepherded them into the dining room, where stood the biggest Christmas tree she had ever seen, it seemed like a climax to the most wonderful party of her life.

There were presents on the tree for all the children, little presents, not embarrassingly expensive—plastic toys for the younger children, balls, marbles, cheap imitation jewelry. Bernie Hope, recognizable under red gown and white whiskers, began with the youngest children, so that

Tessa came near the end. She opened the parcel without excitement. It was the same shape as her cousin Vivienne Ritchie's, whose gaudy brooch she had already been asked to admire. Tessa did not care for jewelry.

Something fluttered to the floor as she unwrapped the expected brooch. Ruth, too old for the Christmas tree but more curious than Tessa about presents, had been leaning over her shoulder and bent to pick it up. "Ooh, Mum," she called, "isn't she lucky? Isn't this just the thing for a bookworm like Tessa?"

She held up a book token. It was clean and new, not one of the screwed-up pieces of cardboard that Tessa had thrown in Mr. Sanderson's face, but it brought back so much that the party had swept out of her mind, the fate of Cinnamon and Nutmeg, as well as the memory of her own rudeness. Nobody else had been given such a valuable present. She was sure that Mr. Sanderson was punishing her, as she deserved, with this reminder of her rudeness.

"Oh, Mr. Sanderson, you shouldn't," she heard Mum say in a voice that was not quite her everyday one. "Come along now, Tessa, say thank you to Mr. Sanderson."

"Thank you," Tessa mumbled, looking at the floor. Her shame made her sound less grateful than the children who had thanked him for their plastic toys.

"That's all right, Tessa." Mr. Sanderson also sounded embarrassed. "I owed it to you."

"Dennis Sanderson!" It was Aunt Helen's voice, but sharpened to an unfamiliar pitch. "You are the most tactless boor of a man!"

"Helen, shush," said Mum, alarmed by the memory of Aunt Helen's threats.

"I will not shush. Cruelty to children is one thing I will not tolerate. Look at the child, Dennis Sanderson, and tell me if you're not the greatest fool that ever was."

Everybody looked at Tessa and she wondered what they saw. Was it clearly written on her face that she wanted to be away from them all, in her little tent with Sam curled up on her feet, to cry and cry because everything was wrong and she had thrown her book tokens at Mr. Sanderson?

"But, Helen . . ." began Mr. Sanderson mildly.

"Don't you 'but Helen' me. You can make any mess you like out of your own life, but you just leave my niece's life alone."

"Helen, you don't know . . ."

"I know everything. Tessa threw a couple of book tokens in your face, as any right-thinking person would— if they couldn't lay their hands on something heavier. So you think you'll make things up with your deservedly guilty conscience by going out and buying the child another book token without having the common sense to see the memories you're bringing back to her. Do you think she wants to see another book token ever again— or your face, for that matter?"

"All right, I admit it," said Mr. Sanderson. "It may have been a tactless way of making my apologies. Now, Helen, do you think we can go on having a Christmas party?"

But Aunt Helen was no longer interested in Christmas parties. She had threatened to tell Dennis Sanderson what she thought of him and now she was worked up to it. "You've no right to keep a pet lamb, let alone a sheep farm," she told him. "That Young Pat's a rogue, and Howarth's a bigger one, and if you weren't too lazy to accept your responsibilities—"

"My dear Helen—"

"I'm not your dear Helen. You'd let those two steal the ground from under your feet before you lifted a hand to stop them. A tissue of lies they concoct and you're too bone lazy to care whether or not they stole your most valuable cow. Do you know how many cows you've got? Or how many you ought to have?"

"Young Pat says . . ."

"Young Pat says," she mimicked. "Dennis Sanderson the lawyer must have been the comedy act of the century if you went about taking the word of every liar and thief as trustingly as you believe those two."

"Helen, please." Several of Mr. Sanderson's guests had gathered up their coats, since the party seemed to have ended and a private argument taken its place, which they could not interrupt even to say good-bye. Mr. Sanderson moved toward them, then turned back to Aunt Helen with a temper that was growing as short as her own.

"You can't pass judgment on people you don't know," he told her. "How long have you been back in Manurima? Two days? Have you spoken to Ted or Pat? Of course you haven't. Hearsay, nothing but hearsay. You've just been listening to children's tales."

"So my daughter and my niece are liars?"

"Typical, that is. You never could follow a logical argument."

"Logical argument? You were bellowing like a bull."

"I bellowed logic—you screamed emotional nonsense."

"If it's emotional to care about the happiness of innocent children—"

"What innocent child have I ever hurt?"

"That one, for a start." Aunt Helen pointed dramatically at Tessa, who wished she could disappear through the floor.

"Helen, please, be reasonable. I didn't take Tessa's calf away from her."

"Oh yes, you did."

"The calf's proven owner took her away. Please try to

get some grasp of the facts even if you can't deduce a reasonable conclusion from them. Logic never was your strong point."

"It certainly wasn't when I got engaged to you."

"I must have been somewhat young and foolish myself."

Jan hung her mother's coat across her shoulders. The last guests had crept away as the argument became more and more personal. Only the Duggans remained and Dad was already at the doorway, trying to shepherd them away. He hated scenes unless they were of his own making. Jan took one of her mother's arms and Mum took the other and they led her quickly away before she could think of her next retort.

At the door Tessa turned and looked back at Mr. Sanderson. She had thought there was nothing she wanted more than to get herself and Aunt Helen away from Riverlea, but when she saw him standing alone by the Christmas tree she was sorry that a man who had planned so much pleasure for others should be left alone and unthanked.

She ran across the room and, looking hard at her feet, blurted out her thanks for a lovely party. Then she looked up at the man she had pitied and saw that he was clutching a branch of the Christmas tree, laughing. Tessa blushed, thinking herself the joke.

"It isn't you, Tessa. You did that charmingly. It's that crazy aunt of yours. She hasn't changed a bit in all these years. Isn't she wonderful?"

"I think she was perfectly beastly, breaking up your party like that."

"It was worth it, Tessa, believe me."

As she turned away he was laughing again.

FOURTEEN

Aunt Helen Goes Trespassing

The day after Christmas was hot and humid. Uncle Alec, his two sons, their wives, and Colin were all invited to a meal that was little less filling than the Christmas dinner of the day before. Afterward, having been chased outside to get some exercise that they were too hot and full to want, the three girls and Colin began a lazy game of French cricket in the deserted orchard. They agreed a dozen times that the next time the person with the bat was caught would be the last, but each time they found it too much effort to think of another game and went on playing.

When Aunt Helen came through the orchard gate, Tessa was so astonished that she let Jan's carelessly thrown ball trickle past the bat and roll against her foot. Aunt Helen was always so well dressed that nobody would have suspected her of owning, much less of wearing, paint-stained pants with one knee torn almost out and a blouse caked with dry paint. The boots on her feet were Mum's and several sizes too big for her.

"I advise you young ladies to get out of your holiday finery," she said. "This is going to be dirty work in more senses than one."

"Explanation, please," said Jan, who was staring almost as hard as her cousins at her transformed mother.

"We're going trespassing, my child, you and I and anyone else who has a taste for adventure and the solution of mysteries. We're going to do for that great booby Dennis Sanderson what he hasn't the gumption to do for him-

174

self, and go over his land with a fine-toothed comb until
we unearth—whatever there is to be unearthed. And if
there isn't something crooked going on there, I'll eat—
I haven't got a hat with me—I'll eat Ted Howarth's un-
mentionable headgear."

Aunt Helen had made up her mind. They pointed out
that people just did not go hunting mysteries on other
people's land and that in any case it was impossible to go
over two thousand acres with a fine-toothed comb on a
sweltering December afternoon on top of a holiday dinner. "If you prefer French cricket," said Aunt Helen,
"that's all right with me, though I can't say I admire your
taste. But I'm going."

In the end, rather than trust her to explore alone, the
girls changed into their oldest clothes and they all crammed
into Aunt Helen's little car. Colin, who knew the geogra-
phy of every farm in the district, sat in front with Aunt
Helen to point out the boundary of Ted Howarth's farm
with Riverlea, which was where she intended to begin her
exploration.

She was out of the car and over the taut barbed-wire
fence while the girls and Colin were still guiltily looking
around, and crossed the turf with strides that were sur-
prisingly long for so small a person, questioning Colin
as she went about the state of the grass, the making of
silage, the health of a flock of sheep. All he could say was,
"Looks awright to me," until Aunt Helen, who had set
her heart on finding something that was all wrong, lapsed
into frustrated silence.

They crossed three paddocks without discovering a sign
to indicate that Riverlea was not a perfectly organized
farm. Then, "Crikey," said Colin as they looked over the
next fence at a dozen nondescript cows. "When did Riverlea take up with stock like that?"

"Strays," said Ruth with prompt common sense. "You know how Dad's always complaining about Mr. Howarth's boundary with us. Why shouldn't it be as bad on this side?"

"Could be," said Colin, but Aunt Helen's suspicions were catching and he ran along the side of the macrocarpa windbreak that divided Mr. Howarth's land from Riverlea. Halfway along he turned to beckon and shout something that they couldn't catch.

Aunt Helen ran forward and the girls plodded behind. By the time they caught up with her she was talking eagerly to Colin beside a brand-new gate in the boundary fence. The logs of two macrocarpa trees that had been cut down to make space for it still littered the ground.

"I must say," said Aunt Helen, "I almost admire their coolness. Calmly letting themselves into the boss's good grazing. Did you ever see anything like it for plain, cold-blooded impudence?"

"Those calves in the next paddock, Colin," said Jan, "would they be Ted Howarth's too?"

Colin took one glance to where Jan was pointing and then went splashing through the mud in the best shoes he had not had time to change. And as he ran he called, "Cinnamon!"

Tessa climbed through the fence as Colin walked toward a scrawny calf with protruding ribs and hanging head which stood alone in a corner of the paddock. It was less than two weeks since the Livestock Show and yet Tessa herself could hardly recognize the sleek prizewinner that Ted Howarth had led away.

Cinnamon, however, still knew Tessa. As she ran past Colin, the calf took a few steps forward and gave a low, unhappy moo. Tessa knelt and held out her arms for

Cinnamon to come to her, as she had so often done in the orchard. Without hesitation, Cinnamon trotted forward.

With her arms around Cinnamon's neck, Tessa looked up at Aunt Helen. "Please," was all she could manage to say.

Jan confidently answered for her mother, "Of course, you must take her. Even I can see that calf's been thoroughly neglected. A man like that's got no right to a calf like Cinnamon."

"Hold on, hold on," said Aunt Helen with sudden caution. "We've got a case to prove. I wouldn't trust Dennis Sanderson to know a Riverlea cow from those multicolored freaks of Howarth's, but he can't deny that Cinnamon is Cinnamon. Don't fret, Tessa. We're getting somewhere now, and I guarantee she'll be out of Howarth's clutches before the day's out."

Aunt Helen turned back toward the road and Jan, Ruth, and Colin followed. Ruth had called back to her several times before Tessa could make herself leave Cinnamon. She walked slowly, with many backward glances, even when Cinnamon was no longer in sight.

When she reached the road, the older girls were already beside Aunt Helen's car. Aunt Helen herself was astride the fence, impatiently directing Colin's clumsy attempts to unhook a barb that had caught in the leg of her pants.

She was still caught there when Mr. Sanderson's blue station wagon pulled up on the road beside her. "What's this then?" Mr. Sanderson called, leaning out of the window. "Trespassers?" His eyes were creased with laughter and from the seat beside him Jenny Wren, crisp and cool in a sleeveless cotton dress, laughed aloud.

As Colin deserted her to stare in alarm at the new-comers, Aunt Helen squirmed around, trying to un-hook herself.

"Do you need help?" asked Mr. Sanderson.

Aunt Helen brushed damp strands of hair from her eyes and scowled at him. "Please don't trouble yourself," she said. "The view from here is excellent."

"But may I remind you that your left leg is trespassing on my property while you admire the view?"

"And as well someone does take the trouble to trespass, as you call it, and find out for you what's happening on your own land."

"Upon which I dutifully say, 'Helen, dear Helen, tell me please, what is happening on my land?' "

It was not easy to be dignified, caught up on the top strand of the fence with only the toe of one boot touching the ground. Aunt Helen did her best. "If you're inter-ested," she said, "your farm manager just happens to be letting off half your best land to his mate. Complete with new gateway for easy access."

"You saw this for yourself?"

"As you could if you ever bothered to leave your pre-cious stereo equipment and your blond schoolma'am and take a stroll across your own property. Presuming, that is, that you know a purebred Jersey from a mixture of Friesian and heaven-knows-what."

Her last words were almost lost in the slamming of the car door behind Mr. Sanderson. Without a word, he climbed the fence and strode across the paddock. Then he paused, hesitated, returned with the same energetic strides to Aunt Helen, and hauled her down from the fence. There was a large three-cornered tear in the leg of her pants as she followed him across the paddock, keeping pace with his angry strides like the farm girl she had been.

Cinnamon was waiting at the fence. She greeted Tessa with a small sad moo.

"Is that . . ." said Mr. Sanderson, and then, when Tessa had climbed through the fence and was kneeling with Cinnamon's bowed head between her hands, "I see it is. And no sign of the little goat I hear you gave him to stop her pining. Well, since Cinnamon is on my land, I'm impounding her here and now as a stray. Will she follow you without a halter, Tessa?"

Tessa nodded, too happy to speak.

"With your approval, of course," Mr. Sanderson told Aunt Helen with a mocking bow.

"Don't play the fool," said Aunt Helen sharply. Then suddenly her voice became serious, even gentle, and the teasing spark left her eyes. "Please, Den, for Tessa's sake if you won't do it for your own, try to act like a responsible landowner. You know Ted Howarth told a pack of lies to get that calf—and now look at the way he treats her. You've got to get her back, Den, and not just for today."

"I know," said Mr. Sanderson. "I know he was lying, but there's nothing I could prove in a court of law. There are the receipts, Helen, signed by my brother; they're not forgeries. I've had them looked at by a handwriting expert. I've seen the cow that's buried on Ted's property —what's left of her, poor thing. She's Princess without a doubt. And all the evidence we have proves her and therefore her calf to be Howarth's property. Helen, I just don't know what else I can do."

Aunt Helen took his arm. "Come on, Den," she said. "Let's get back to Riverlea and go over those papers

again and see what the old firm can do. We used to work
pretty well together, you and I."

As Aunt Helen and Mr. Sanderson walked away together, Ruth said, "Come on, Tessa. You heard what Mr.
Sanderson said. Will she follow you?"

Tessa nodded and walked toward the gate. Cinnamon
stood a moment looking unhappy and then bounded forward with an indignant moo as if determined that this
time Tessa would not desert her.

"Look, Jan! Look, Ruth!" Tessa called as Cinnamon
trotted through the gate at her heels. "Did you ever see?
Isn't she the most clever calf in the world?"

Jan turned. Her mother and Mr. Sanderson were out of
sight. "She's lovely, Tessa," she said vaguely. Then, with
real enthusiasm, "You girls, did you see that? Tessa,
Ruth, wouldn't it be wonderful if they got married after
all these years? If I came to live at Riverlea!"

"It's terribly romantic," said Ruth. "And listen, Tessa,
if Cinnamon really is Mr. Sanderson's and if Jan's right
and people as old as that can sort of fall back into love
and get married, then Cinnamon will be Jan's, sort of.
That won't be as bad as Mr. Howarth, will it?"

Tessa looked jealously at her cousin's happy face. If
Aunt Helen married Mr. Sanderson, Jan would have the
things that mattered to her—chess, music, Mr. Sanderson
for a father. Why should she have Cinnamon too? Though
it would be better to think of Cinnamon with Jan than
with Ted Howarth.

Both cars were gone by the time they reached the
road. So was Colin. Tessa led the way to Riverlea at a
speed which Jan, Ruth, and Cinnamon all found too
much for a hot afternoon. But Tessa, if she could have
persuaded Cinnamon to keep up with her, would have
run all the way. The road was dangerous; at any moment

Ted Howarth might come by and claim his calf. Cinnamon was panting like a dog when they entered the Riverlea drive, and neither Ruth nor Jan had breath enough to complain that they were exhausted. Tessa was hot and tired too, but scarcely aware of it. For the moment she and Cinnamon were safely together and she dared not think beyond the present moment.

Colin had been stationed to show them to Young Pat's office, a dingy little box of a room beside the tractor shed. It was crammed with files and the walls were almost covered with rosettes and certificates won by several generations of Riverlea cows. With seven people and one calf, the room was cramped and stuffy, with scarcely space to move or breathe.

Aunt Helen and Mr. Sanderson were searching through the piles of papers that littered an ancient roll-top desk. As Tessa was pushed by the crowd against Aunt Helen's elbow, Aunt Helen waved a small open book above her head. "I've got it!" she almost shrieked.

Everybody pushed as close as they could until Aunt Helen was almost crushed between Mr. Sanderson on one side and Tessa on the other, "What is it, Helen?" asked Mr. Sanderson. Perhaps in the crush there was nowhere for his arm to go except around her waist.

"The farm's receipt book," said Aunt Helen. "Look, Den. The top page gets torn out and given as the receipt, but a second page with a carbon copy of the top stays in the book."

"In other words," said Mr. Sanderson, "a perfectly normal receipt book."

"Right. But just look here. In a perfectly normal receipt book the number of each receipt is printed on the receipt and the carbon copy, and the numbers follow in sequence. But here we have two blank pages. The receipts have been torn off but there's no carbon copy. Couldn't Young Pat . . ."

"Yes, he could," said Mr. Sanderson, catching her unspoken thought. "Write in the old numbers, trace Graham's signature from an old receipt. Nothing easier on this thin paper."

"And that means," said Aunt Helen, "that somewhere there are carbon copies of the receipts with the number he used, recording something quite different."

"Unless he tore them out," said Jan.

"Then I'd like to hear him explain a coincidence like that," said Mr. Sanderson. "Come on, Jan, there's a shelf of old receipt books right behind you. Look for 1467 and 1512."

Jan looked through the dusty shelf of old receipt books once and then began all over again. Everyone else was silent, waiting. Then, as Jan began a third time, Jenny Wren bustled over to help her. Jan gave her an unwelcoming look and got on with the search.

"Are you sure you got the numbers right?" asked Jenny Wren when, to Jan's silent annoyance, she had checked each book as if the search were a classroom exercise and Jan a backward pupil.

"Numbers 1467 and 1512," Mr. Sanderson repeated. "I've brooded over those receipts until the numbers got burned in my memory. Aren't they there, Jan?"

"Neither of them," said Jenny Wren.

"They'd be in the same book, Dennis," said Jan with a black look at Jenny Wren. "There's 1350 to 1450 and 1550 to 1650, but the book between's missing."

"Can I help?" asked a pleasant voice from the doorway. They all turned to see Young Pat leaning against the doorpost, his hands in his pockets and a friendly smile on his face. They were in his office, the smile said, but he was ready to forgive them all and welcome them as guests. "Is there something I can find for you, Mr. Sanderson?" he asked.

"Yes, Pat, I think there is," said Mr. Sanderson without returning the smile. "One of the old receipt books appears to be missing. What were the numbers it covered again, Jan?"

Jan told him.

Young Pat repeated the numbers thoughtfully. "That'll be before my time, I fancy. I understood all the old books were on the shelf there. Don't think I've had cause to look through them myself."

"I think you had cause to look through this one, Pat," said Mr. Sanderson. "Or do receipt numbers 1467 and 1512 mean nothing to you?"

"Oh, I follow you now," said Young Pat, beaming at them all as if he expected them to applaud his quickness. "Those two receipts of Ted's are bothering you again. No, I've never had cause to look for the copies when Ted had the originals. Shall I run over and borrow them for you, Mr. Sanderson?"

Young Pat was so eager to help that he was halfway through the door before the sharpness of Mr. Sanderson's "Pat!" made him turn.

"Yes, Mr. Sanderson?"

"Just come back here a moment and look at this." Mr. Sanderson picked up the receipt book which lay on the desk, still open at the two blank pages. "Can you explain this?"

Young Pat took the book from him and studied the two pages. "Ah yes, Mr. Sanderson," he said, "I'd been meaning to tell you about that. My fault entirely, I'm afraid. I must have put the carbon paper in upside down and didn't notice until I'd written out two receipts."

"But you remember what the receipts were for?"

"That's the awful part, Mr. Sanderson; I haven't a clue. But I'm sure they can't have been for anything big or I'd remember, wouldn't I? I'm really most sorry and I'll see it doesn't happen again. Shall I go and get those receipts for you now?"

"Thank you, Pat, but I think we should check our own copies of those Howarth receipts. Suppose my brother also put the carbon paper in upside down. It could be a serious matter to find that we are without copies of such important documents."

"No doubt you, being a lawyer and all, would know best, Mr. Sanderson," said Young Pat without enthusiasm. But he joined in the search with such energy that Ruth whispered to Tessa, "I do think some people have nasty, suspicious minds," looking to where Aunt Helen and Mr. Sanderson searched together through a stack of dusty files.

Colin went up to Mr. Sanderson and whispered something.

"Looking at that floorboard, is he?" said Aunt Helen in a loud voice. "And a rough, loose-looking one it is. We're a rotten lot of detectives. Well done, Colin."

She crossed the room and, before anyone else had done more than stare, had the floorboard up and was pulling something from the hole beneath.

Mr. Sanderson leaped across the room, just in time to get his arms around Young Pat as he backed through the doorway. Colin was close behind him and grabbed Young Pat's arm. He made no further attempt to escape, but stood watching as all eyes were turned back to Aunt Helen.

She turned the pages of a receipt book. "Number 1467 —is that right, Den?—ten two-toothed Romney ewes sold to a Mr. Stewart of Taumaranui. And number 1512—behold, our friend from Taumaranui again—a Corriedale ram this time. Now let's see you talk your way out of this one, Pat."

Young Pat squirmed between his captors and said nothing.

"Here's some more interesting reading," said Jan, who had taken her mother's place at the hole and brought out a second book. "Young Pat's own receipt book, or his rent book, to be more accurate. It appears that we missed something. Ted Howarth's been paying rent for five paddocks in all."

"All right, all right," said Young Pat, "so you've seen the paddocks. And the cow thing; I suppose those receipts give that away too. I told Ted we'd never get away with it, but he had his heart set on the calf ever since that Sunday when everybody was admiring her, and what could a man do? It was that wretched Princess that started it all. If only she hadn't taken it into her stupid head to wander off and lose her silly self. . . .

"It was after you'd been at me about the broken fence, Mr. Sanderson. I just hadn't got around to mending it or moving the cows, and then Princess, of all animals, went missing. I didn't dare tell you because it was a good week since you'd told me to mend the fence, so I told my friend, Ted. Him and me and his two biggest boys searched the bush all one day without seeing a living thing except that old goat that Ted shot. He treated that outing like a holiday and I soon knew why he was feeling so chirpy. He had a hold over me after that: unless I rented him those paddocks, he'd tell the boss about Princess. Rent, not give, you'll notice, but dirt cheap, of course, so that if anything came out, I looked like the real villain.

"I also had to go along with him when he made up his

mind to get Cinnamon. And some job it was, too. I used to belong to a drama club where I worked before and I was reckoned pretty good, but I never had a job like teaching that young Billy his lines. I sweated over that kid, and his father and Warren weren't much better. Still, we put on a pretty good performance in the end. Too good for you, eh, Mr. Sanderson?"

"But not quite good enough for Colin today, eh, Pat?" Mr. Sanderson imitated his tone. "Well, thank you at least, Pat, for a frank and full confession. You'll have to learn, won't you, to keep clear of the Ted Howarths of this world."

"Dennis Sanderson!" Aunt Helen exclaimed. "You're not letting him off, just like that!"

"You're really too generous for your own good sometimes, Dennis," said Jenny Wren, smiling at him.

"Generous, my foot!" said Aunt Helen. "Blackmail or no, that man conspired with Ted Howarth and his abominable offspring to steal a child's pet."

"And cruelty to children is one thing you will not tolerate," quoted Mr. Sanderson. "I'm not exactly an admirer of it myself, Helen dear."

"Then do something. Call the police. Tessa, it's your calf they stole. You tell this man that you want the villains punished."

"What would you suggest then, Tessa?" asked Mr. Sanderson.

Tessa looked at the man who stood between Mr. Sanderson and Colin and could scarcely recognize the handsome cousin she had once admired. She would have been sorry for him if she had not remembered poor neglected Cinnamon—and Nutmeg, still with the Howarths, her own, now purposeless, gift. "I'd rather he wasn't in charge of the Riverlea herd now that Cinnamon's in it, if you don't mind, Mr. Sanderson," she timidly suggested.

"He won't be," Mr. Sanderson promised. "You can pack now and get out, Pat. A month's pay in lieu of notice should be sufficient, I think." He raised his voice to check an interruption from Aunt Helen. "Unfortunately when I've deducted the rent you owe me for the land you've been subletting, your pay envelope's going to look very empty. I'll send you the bill for the rest later."

"Fair enough, I suppose," muttered Young Pat, "except that, if you don't mind me saying so, Mr. Sanderson, is it quite fair that I have to lose a good job and pay all that money if Ted Howarth is going to get off scot-free?"

"Fair?" said Aunt Helen. "It's the unfairest thing I've ever heard of that you should get away without being punished. You ought to be jailed."

"Helen, calm down," said Mr. Sanderson. "Yes, I do mind your having the impudence to make any complaints at all, Pat, and if I hear any more, I'll hand you over to your Aunt Helen and her sense of justice. As for Ted Howarth, he's had a lot of bad luck recently. First there's the expensive business of mending all his boundary fences rather than face a court case that he hasn't a hope of winning. And last time I passed his place it was crawling with Department of Agriculture men, out hunting gorse. That means a substantial fine as well as the expense and labor of getting rid of the stuff. Ted may never develop a conscience about stealing children's pets, but he's certainly learning the price of hurting Joe Duggan's daughter. I'd get out quickly, Pat, if I were you, before Joe realizes the part you've played in all this. And thank your lucky stars that both Tessa and I happen to be in a very forgiving mood today."

He smiled at Tessa and she wondered if his reunion with Aunt Helen after nearly twenty years felt as good as hers with Cinnamon after nearly two weeks. And now she had proof of Dad's concern for her. She returned his smile happily.

"Yes, Mr. Sanderson, thank you, Mr. Sanderson," said Young Pat, and as Mr. Sanderson and Colin both stood back as if no longer on guard, he backed hastily through the door.

"Now," said Mr. Sanderson, "I've still got a bit of business to attend to, so why don't you people make yourselves at home? Jan, you know your way around the kitchen. How about you girls making a cup of tea? Have a look through the refrigerator and see what you can dig up. There must be some Christmas cake still left somewhere."

Jenny Wren, who also knew her way around the Riverlea kitchen, did not seem very pleased at being left on the veranda with Aunt Helen and Colin while the girls made the tea. When they returned with their tray, Aunt Helen was chatting brightly to a very glum young woman while Colin, who had found a calf halter somewhere, was grazing Cinnamon on the smooth Riverlea lawn.

They had almost finished their tea before Mr. Sanderson returned, heralded by Colin's teacup somersaulting across the lawn and smashing on the gravel. He had been holding Cinnamon's rope and a piece of Christmas cake in one hand and his cup and saucer in the other, and now stumbled forward, dragged by Cinnamon's convulsive bound toward Mr. Sanderson, who was leading Nutmeg on a length of grubby clothesline.

Nutmeg shot forward and the watchers on the veranda laughed as the man and the boy were towed helplessly toward each other.

"Let them go, Colin," called Mr. Sanderson, suiting the action to the word. "My arms are almost torn out of their sockets. They won't wander, will they, Tessa?"

"I don't think so." Tessa's eyes shone. "Oh, I'm so glad you got her away from those Howarths," she cried.

"Nothing easier, Tessa. Can you see Ted Howarth wanting to keep an animal that didn't bring in any money?"

"You won't feel like that, will you, Mr. Sanderson? I mean, I don't suppose you really want a pet goat, but Cinnamon does. You can see." She pointed to the friends who, both released, chased each other around and around Colin. Then a new thought struck her. "Maybe you can take care of Nutmeg, Jan. In the holidays, anyway."

"Of course I will," said Jan.

"A pet goat in an apartment?" asked Mr. Sanderson.

"Don't be dense," Aunt Helen called down from the veranda. "Don't you know a matchmaker when you see one?"

"I really must be going," said Jenny Wren suddenly, putting her teacup back on the tray with a rattle.

"Oh, must you?" said Mr. Sanderson, politely, his eyes fixed on Aunt Helen.

"And I'm afraid I really must go home the first thing tomorrow morning."

"Do come again," said Mr. Sanderson, but it did not sound as though his heart were in it.

Jenny Wren marched off, the heels of her sandals clicking on the gravel drive. They heard the engine of her car cough into life and splutter several times, as if it shared its owner's mood, before it roared angrily away.

Mr. Sanderson did not seem to notice she had gone. He appeared to be wrapped up in thought. "When's your birthday, Tessa?" he asked abruptly.

"June," said Tessa, puzzled.

"That won't do. And Christmas is over. Helen, shall we make it an engagement present in reverse?"

"You haven't proposed to her," Jan reminded him.

"Oh, I went through all that nearly twenty years ago. I've never proposed to you, Jan. Will you accept me as a stepfather?"

"Too right!"

"Then that's settled," said Mr. Sanderson with a grin at Aunt Helen, who opened her mouth to speak and seemed to find nothing to say. "Now back to business. An engagement present in reverse then, Tessa, how's that? From Helen Freeman and Dennis Sanderson to Tessa Duggan, one Jersey heifer calf, to be registered at my expense as Riverlea Cinnamon out of Riverlea Princess by—I'm not sure who her father was, but it'll be in my brother's papers—the real ones."

"Oh, Mr. Sanderson, you can't. She's too valuable," said Ruth.

"Oh, I don't know, Ruth," said Mr. Sanderson. "Look at it this way. I was fool enough to employ a farm manager who lost Princess and hadn't the courage to tell me and organize a proper search. The calf only survived because of Tessa's care—and Colin's. And for that matter, she'd be Ted Howarth's property still if your Aunt Helen knew how to mind her own business and stay in her own backyard. I've so little claim to Cinnamon that, when you come to think of it, it almost seems a nerve for me to give her away. There now, Ruth, you've made me confess everything and ruin my chance of winning a reputation for generosity."

"If it didn't sound like Tessa's Jenny Wren," said Aunt Helen, "I'd say you were the most generous man I know."

"Do say it all the same," said Mr. Sanderson.

"I'll do more than that. By way of reward I'll insist on helping you interview your next farm manager."

"Yes, do," said Mr. Sanderson, taking the veranda steps two at a time. "May I present the one candidate for the job, trained by six months of solid study and picking the brains of a knowledgeable sheep man called Pat Duggan. Mr. Dennis Sanderson at your service, madam."

"Let's get home, you kids," said Ruth.

"Yes," said Jan, aiming her words with a laugh at her mother and Mr. Sanderson. "The company around here is much too childish for us."

It was a long, hot walk, but nobody minded. They let Cinnamon and Nutmeg set the pace, pausing at times while they grazed at the roadside.

"And I'll tell you another thing," said Jan suddenly as they sat lazily among the tall grass during one of their breaks. "I'll bet anything you like that now she's lost her chance of becoming a sheep farmer's wife, Jenny Wren won't stay in Manurima any longer than she has to. In fact, I wouldn't be surprised if you found yourself with a new teacher at the beginning of next term."

Tessa laid her head against Cinnamon's thin side. She had not thought a moment ago that she could be happier, but she was. Suddenly she jumped up. "But Dad doesn't know about Cinnamon yet. Come on, you kids, hurry up, please. He never got his Riverlea bull, but won't he be pleased to have a real registered Riverlea heifer! Both of us, because it doesn't matter that she's registered in my name when it's for our farm."